GAZOOKA

GWYN THOMAS

Gwyn Thomas was born in the Rhondda Valley in 1913. He studied French and Spanish at Oxford and spent time in Spain in the early 1930s. Returning home, he obtained part-time lecturing jobs and later worked for the National Council of Social Service across northern England. In 1940, he became a schoolteacher, first in Cardigan and then in Barry. He retired from that profession in 1962 to work full-time as a writer and broadcaster. He wrote extensively across several genres including essays, short stories, novels and plays, and was widely translated. His fictional works include *The Dark Philosophers* (1946), *Alone to the Alone* (1947) and *All Things Betray Thee* (1949), the prize-winning drama *The Keep* (1962), and an autobiography, *A Few Selected Exits* (1968). Gwyn Thomas was given the Honour for Lifetime Achievement by Arts Council Wales in 1976. He died in 1981.

GAZOOKA

GWYN THOMAS

Parthian, Cardigan SA43 1ED
www.parthianbooks.com
© Gwyn Thomas
Print ISBN: 978-1-914595-72-1
Cover Design: Syncopated Pandemonium
Typeset by Elaine Sharples
Printed by 4edge
Published with the financial support of the Books Council of Wales
British Library Cataloguing in Publication Data
A cataloguing record for this book is available from the British Library.
Printed on FSC accredited paper

INTRODUCTION

I

Gazooka is Gwyn Thomas's most enduring story. It first appeared in 1957, when the writer was at the height of his powers. Since his debut with *The Dark Philosophers* in 1946, there had been eight published novels, a volume of short stories, writing for magazines, newspapers, and for broadcast, and the English Stage Company was pressing for a play to perform at the Royal Court Theatre in London. All this whilst teaching the rudiments of French and Spanish to Barry schoolboys. 'The resilience of Mr Gwyn Thomas is remarkable,' observed the *Daily News* at the time, 'by all rights he should be drying up.' In little more than a decade, Gwyn had caught up with the equally prolific Rhys Davies, that other Rhondda master of fiction. Contemporaries expressed their jealousy, as Kingsley Amis did in his correspondence with Philip Larkin, or embraced such comparisons as were made by critics. When the *Daily Telegraph* likened V. S. Naipaul to a 'West Indian Gwyn Thomas' in a review of *The Mystic Masseur* (1957), for example, the future Nobel laureate immediately wrote home to tell his parents that the connection had been made. And, in a review published in *The Spectator*, Francis

Wyndham paid the ultimate compliment by likening the language of *Gazooka* to that employed by Nelson Algren in his *A Walk On The Wildside* (1957). 'This type of American writing,' Wyndham said, 'has much in common with the Welsh.'

As was often the case, Gwyn worked on *Gazooka* over several years, recycling and refining different sources, including radio play scripts and previously published short stories, to create the final product. The novella, the title story of *Gazooka And Other Stories* published by Victor Gollancz, marked the culmination of a decade of creative development and is amongst the very best of the fables set in Meadow Prospect and the Windy Way – the fictional Rhondda communities which share many of their features with the Porth and Cymmer of Gwyn's childhood. The wider geography is that of Glamorgan: the County Keep brings to mind Cardiff Gaol; Birchtown evokes Pontypridd; and Aberclydach serves as a nod to Blaenclydach. That village set in a valley spur just to the west of Tonypandy was the birthplace not only of Rhys Davies but also of Gwyn's adolescent hero, the novelist, county councillor, trade unionist, hunger marcher, and communist, Lewis Jones.

The oldest passages in the text, including the finale, derive from 'Then Came We Singing' which appeared in *Coal*, the National Coal Board's staff magazine, in February 1948. It was here that Gwyn introduced the jazz band into his fiction for the first time, inventing outlandish but true-to-life names like the Ystradcynon Toreadors, the Tredomen

Janissaries, and the Aberclydach Sheikhs. All three bands recur in *Gazooka*. The cast is enormous: there are thirty-seven named individuals ranging from the ironmonger Ephraim Humphries and the Italian café owner, Pablo Tasso, to the quack herbalist, Kitchener Caney, and the local undertaker, Goronwy Mayer. Some of these characters were invented for the stories published in *Coal* between 1948 and 1950; others were created for the novels published by Victor Gollancz, such as *The World Cannot Hear You* (1951) and *The Stranger At My Side* (1954); and still more emerged from the radio plays commissioned by the BBC in the early 1950s. Personalities of a similar type – albeit not, as biographer Michael Parnell once argued, a prototype – can also be found in *The Thinker and the Thrush*, a comic novel in the Meadow Prospect mode written in the 1940s but published posthumously only in 1988.

The first character we encounter in *Gazooka* is Gomer Gough the Gavel, a nickname earned for his role as chairman of the local debating society aka the Discussion Group. Gough's debut had been in 'Tomorrow I Shall Miss You Less', published in *Coal* in December 1950. In that earlier story, we are treated to an amusing portrait of a man who wears a 'creaking blue suit' and is prone to 'apocalyptic forecasts' but who is otherwise an 'unfailing champion in the heavyweight class of dialecticians.' Such was Gwyn's enthusiasm for Gough that he returned multiple times across several stories published throughout the 1950s and 1960s. He tends to be seen in the company of Edwin Pugh and Cynlais Coleman. The latter, known by his nickname 'the Comet', was a Powderhall runner accused by his neighbours of 'doing to morals what Fawkes had tried to do for parliament.' In Gough's last outing, in 'The Comeback' published in *Punch* in 1963, we learn that he 'played a surprisingly gay flute for so ponderous a debater' and was deputy conductor of the Meadow Prospect Silver Jubilee Band.

The woman selected to play Carmen by the members of the Meadow Prospect Toreadors is Moira Hallam. She is a survivor from the original short story, 'Then Came We Singing', and likewise appears elsewhere, always as an alluring archetype of the operatic soprano. In the *Punch* fable 'The Foot and the Snare' published in 1954, she is described as 'famous for appearing in fleshly seductive roles that got the boys spinning and the chapels blinking.' Indeed, she is said to have performed as Salome and as Madame Pompadour. In the 1948 version of this story, again in the guise of Carmen, she appears dressed in a crimson shawl, her dark hair formed into ringlets which drape across her brow, and there is a rose in her mouth destined to be awarded to a princely bullfighter. But nerves get the better of Moira Hallam and she 'nibbled the stem of her rose too long and too fiercely, and for all the jaunty lasciviousness of her hip-swing, we could see she was worried at the prospect of winding up with a stomach full of petals.' A Rosa Ponselle or a Maria Callas, alas, she is not.

This rich cast mirrors those to be found in Damon Runyon's stories set in New York City and amply illustrates

Gwyn's embrace of what he called 'Rhondda Runyonism' – a sympathetic reworking of the American original for the South Walian context, but never as a parody. The easiest way of seeing this common thread is the use of nickname. Erasmus John, the local auctioneer in Meadow Prospect, is known as 'the Going Gone', for instance, Peredur Parry, the unemployment officer, is called 'the Pittance', Naboth Jinks, chairman of the allotment holders union, is known as 'the pinks', and the coalowner Colonel Mathews is referred to as 'the Moloch.' That is, a figure from the Hebrew Bible who demands great sacrifices from the people. Runyon similarly gives his characters nicknames like 'the Dude' or 'the Brain' – the latter based on Arnold Rothstein, the gangster said to have fixed baseball's World Series in 1919 and whom F. Scott Fitzgerald called Meyer Wolfshiem in *The Great Gatsby* – and then sets them off on madcap adventures in the dark, grimy streets of Manhattan. It is a cinematic motif, to be sure, characteristic of the hard-boiled, pulp fiction of the 1930s and 1940s, but one that reflects the demands of writing episodically for newspapers and magazines.

Gwyn first encountered Damon Runyon through BBC radio adaptations of 'Bloodhounds of Broadway' and 'Butch Minds the Baby' broadcast in the summer of 1939. These radio plays were given a second airing in 1945 before the launch, in 1946, of 'Laugh These Off', a more regular slot on the Home Service for dramatised extracts from the comic writing of Runyon, Ogden Nash, and James Thurber. They gave Gwyn a model of humorous writing with serious intentions, a model which he willingly adapted. This American-style dark comedy ultimately replaced an altogether more serious idiom with which he had started out, an idiom evident in *Sorrow For Thy Sons*, which was written in the mid-1930s but not published until 1986, and in *All Things Betray Thee* (1949). As he explained to viewers of the BBC's *Bookstand* in 1962:

> When I decided to use this material [irony, contradiction, absurdity] in fiction, I was faced with a very, very great problem. I was living in a society so complacent that it would not readily accept the material that I was using. Quite apart from the fact that there was a fad of disliking literature that came out of mining valleys because they are damnable and undesirable places. But the very idiom of these people, the kind of apostolic, evangelical note that they struck was certainly out of tune with the prevailing English idiom of the time, which was restrained, gentlemanly, indirect.

American pulp fiction provided the way forward. 'Runyon was dealing with an environment quite as repellent, quite as incredible in its way,' Gwyn explained, 'as the one I had inherited in South Wales.' Broadway thus gained a cousin in the Windy Way.

II

Having found his idiom, Gwyn was able to lift events from the recent South Walian past and turn them into the setting for a different kind of underworld, a society and a culture in which the people were in a 'ferment of discontent.' And so *Gazooka* is set, appropriately, during the turbulence of 1926, the year of the General Strike and a nine-month-long miners' lockout. The story tells of a mining community coming together to form a jazz band to perform at a carnival. As ever, surface events mask a much deeper examination, one rooted in a fizzing combination of the fictive impulses of the novelist and the empirical concentration of the historian. 'On the history of the Gazooka,' wrote the critic and fellow novelist Roy Perrott in 1960, 'Mr Gwyn Thomas, the novelist, is an expert.' Eric Hobsbawm, in the guise of the *New Statesman*'s jazz critic, Francis Newton, made a similar point a couple of years earlier. Gwyn was drawn to the music, to the colour, and above all to the imagery of the jazz bands with their dress up uniforms. Folks took on the character of gauchos, toreadors, nightingales, Russian nutcrackers, Arabian sheikhs, American cowboys, and French onion sellers. 'It wasn't safe to hang up a decent pair of curtains in those days,' he wrote, 'you'd have them whipped to make a uniform.'

The jazz bands were themselves heavily influenced by cinema and by the fanciful, romantic characters who appeared on screen. In fact, if there is a thirty-eighth character present in *Gazooka*, it is the Italian American film star and heartthrob, Rudolph Valentino. At least one of his films is referenced directly in the text: *Blood and Sand* released in 1922 – a tale of a Spanish bullfighter who falls in love with a childhood friend called Carmen. But there are other films referenced more implicitly. The popularity of sheikhs as characters for the bands reflects another of Valentino's films of the period, namely *The Sheikh* released in 1921. A sequel, *The Son of the Sheikh*, released five years later, arrived in Britain in the wake of Valentino's early death on 23 August 1926. Whereas cinema provided costumed imagery, popular music provided aspects of the repertoire performed by the bands at carnivals and competitions. In this respect, the slow march version of 'The Sheik of Araby' played by the Aberclydach Sheikhs, the opponents of the Meadow Prospect Toreadors, deserves comment. The tune was very popular on both sides of the Atlantic in the 1920s and recorded multiple times – such was its Jazz Age prominence that, as Gwyn knew, Scott Fitzgerald quoted an entire verse in *The Great Gatsby*.

Many of the other musical references which appear in *Gazooka* are more traditional, reflecting the contemporary fusion of marching band staples like 'Colonel Bogey', 'Rule Britannia', and 'Anchors Aweigh' with well-known operatic and oratorio fare like the funeral march from Handel's *Saul* and the Toreador's Song from Bizet's *Carmen*, popular hymns including 'Abide with Me' and 'Ar Hyd Yr Nos', and music hall fare. The latter is signalled by the chorus line 'I'm one of the nuts of Barcelona' of *Barcelona: Indigo, Yes Indigo*, a one-step written by Tolchard Evans and released in 1926. Its lyrics are suitably madcap and the melody recalls George Formby Sr's 1909 record Plink Plonk (The Skin of a Spanish Onion):

> I'm one of the nuts from Barcelona,
> I plink-a de plonk, I casa-bionk,
> I dance-a de dance with fine Polona,
> She shake-a de hip, I get-a de pip,
> Round at the bar I order wine,
> Half-a de mo I'm feeling fine,
> Light-a de fag, the old Woodbine,
> Order a cab for half past nine.
> I'm one of the nuts from Barcelona,
> Where skies are blue as indigo,
> Indigo—YES—Indigo.

The exception to this soundscape is George Gershwin's *Swanee*, which is on the lips of the narrator as *Gazooka* opens. The artist Gwyn had in mind when he wrote the story was Al Jolson, who recorded the song several times over the course of his career and was closely identified with its performance. But for contemporary readers there was another vocalist who might also come to mind: Judy Garland. She took on the mantle in the 1950s, after Jolson's death, when the song was added to the repertoire that she performed in *A Star Is Born* (1954). Her version was current when *Gazooka* was published.

III

What we have in this story, then, is a richly ambitious portrait of a society and a culture which has absorbed external influences and turned them into something original. It was that originality combined with the universalism of Gwyn's comedy that turned a one-off short story published in the staff magazine of the National Coal Board into one of the BBC's most successful radio programmes of the early 1950s. Without those broadcasts there would be no novella. Gwyn was approached initially to write a stand-alone feature for the Welsh Home Service. This was broadcast on 11 January 1952. The programme's full title, 'Gazooka: A Rhondda Reminiscence', captured the underlying motivation. The South Wales of the early 1950s was changing, becoming a land more of factories and cars than of coal mines and trams. The National Coal Board was five years old, the National Health Service a mere four, and for a few more weeks Britain was ruled by the ailing George VI. As for the novelist, well, he was eighteen months shy of his fortieth birthday, an event certain to make anyone stop and reflect on what was and what might have been.

That initial Welsh broadcast was popular enough, but nothing could quite prepare Gwyn or the BBC for the reaction to the UK-wide airing from London a year later. A first outing on 5 January 1953 led to no fewer than three repeats, all before the end of the year, together with international airings in Canada and New Zealand. The London broadcasts could be picked up by listeners in Denmark,

Ireland, the Netherlands, and Norway, as well. To accompany the release of *Gazooka And Other Stories* in 1957, the Welsh Home Service provided a further repeat of the feature. Those listening were bowled over. J. C. Trewin, radio critic of *The Listener*, told his readers that *Gazooka* 'sticks in the mind now as one of the most summoning features for a long time ... once heard [it] will revive itself often in the grateful memory.' Trewin was not alone in this view. Lionel Hale in the *Observer* confessed that he 'went on his knees with a will to the BBC for playing it' and Maurice Wiggin, writing in the *Sunday Times*, declared 'this hilarious piece of fun' had 'made most of the English comedy programmes sound forced, poverty-stricken, lame.'

As a production for radio, *Gazooka* was the co-creation of Gwyn and producer Elwyn Evans, who was then based at the BBC in Cardiff. Everything was performed live in the studio. The musical numbers called for in the script led to a search for a real gazooka band and then, when that hunt proved unsuccessful – Evans was told by one band that the required pieces were not part of their repertoire – there was a rushed purchase of a dozen instruments from a city centre music shop. These were placed in the hands of Gwyn, as the story's narrator, and the rest of the cast. One observer later reported that 'cast and author seized them [the gazookas] with avidity and practised hard and noisily.' By comparing the radio script with the short stories and the novella, we can observe the development of the narrative from aural to visual imagination. Indeed, what could be captured for the listener in a stage direction had to be spelled out in a novella to give the reader the same imagined image. Likewise, timing on radio was everything. But in this case, the reworking turned an effective piece of narration into a marvellously evocative and lyrical passage, one which left the reader in no doubt as to where they were, and when.

This is how the opening of 'Gazooka: A Rhondda Reminiscence' is scripted:

FAINTLY, DRUMS AND GAZOOKAS PLAYING 'SWANEE'. THE SOUND APPROACHES GROWS LOUDER, THEN FADES AWAY.

NARRATOR: And to my ears, whenever that tune is played, the brave ghosts march again and my ears are full of the wonder they knew in the months of that long, idle, sunlit summer of 1926.

And this is how the novella begins:

Somewhere outside my window a child is whistling. He is walking fast down the hill and whistling. The tune on his lips is 'Swanee'... the sound of it promotes a roaring life inside my ears. Whenever I hear it, brave ghosts, in endless procession, march again. My eyes are full of the wonder they knew in the months of that long, idle, beautifully lit summer of 1926.

Notice the subtle changes of language, the 'long, idle, sunlit summer' gains in rhythm and cadence with the exchange of 'beautifully lit summer.' There are similar amendments throughout, as the novella form asserts itself over the building blocks of a radio script and a group of short stories. This is the creative habit of a dedicated professional, a writer committed to the process of perfecting an idea but never averse to trying it out in different contexts along the way.

Gwyn revisited the story for a fourth time in 1965 for the television Wales and the West documentary, *Return to the Rhondda*. This saw four prominent celebrities – Donald Houston, Stanley Baker, Tommy Farr, and Gwyn himself – head back to the valley of their childhood and pass comment on its influence, its history, its society, its culture, even its jokes, and then reflect on how things had changed. Gwyn certainly had changed – he was in his mid-fifties, retired from teaching, no longer writing novels, and firmly detached from the Rhondda of his childhood. At the start of his sequence, he gives a reading from the opening of *Gazooka*, the novella, as archive photographs and footage of terraced streets are shown on screen. It is an affecting piece of television, a *son et lumière* for a lost world. But not a lamented one, certainly not for Stanley Baker who, in the remains of the Ferndale Colliery which had cost his father his leg, turns to the camera to say that this is 'my idea of hell.'

There was to be one final visit to this subject in 1976, the fiftieth anniversary of the General Strike, this time at the invitation of the BBC. *Gazooka Summer* aired on BBC Two on 4 August. We see a new generation learning to play the gazooka, the scales dictated not by classical music notation but by the tonic sol-fa of the old choral tradition. 'They are the chicks of a great eagle which rose in the skies over South Wales fifty years ago,' Gwyn says in voice over. Soon we see the modern version of the jazz bands, as they pass through increasingly car-filled streets. Their uniforms are no longer haphazard manufactures created from curtains and tea cosies but instead mimic those of an American band. They are led from the front by a signaller armed with a mace. 'I cannot ever look at them or hear them,' Gwyn explains,

> without being utterly pervaded by one strong, inde-structible memory of the past because it is one of the great ironies of our time, that this thing, this playing of gazookas by organised bands actually emerged from one of the most sombre, dangerous moments in our past: 1926. And indeed it is rather nice to think when looking at these bands of young people that they are throwing flowers, in a way, very acceptable flowers, over what was one of the most decisive wounds in our social experience.

Of course, the jazz band could not outrun coal's demise. Once the mines shut, so the gazookas themselves fell silent.

IV

A few years ago, I had the chance to lead a workshop about carnival. The school I was working with had already been teaching its eager classes of six- and seven-year-olds about the colourful Brazilian affair with masks and streamers and samba dancing. I was asked about local traditions that could be incorporated into the lesson and to the exhibition that was planned for parents at the end of term. I seized the chance to tell pupils and teachers alike about the jazz bands of 1926 and tracked down some plastic kazoos for us all to play. The sound of the nursery rhyme 'The Grand Old Duke of York' being hummed through a piece of resonant plastic was as would be expected but, in that moment, marching around the bandstand in Ynysangharad War Memorial Park in Pontypridd, we were repeating a piece of history. A history that no-one else in the workshop that day knew.

As we approach the centenary of 1926, there can be no more authentic way of understanding why communities across South Wales – and further afield, for instance in Northumberland and County Durham – created the jazz bands, than by reading Gwyn Thomas's *Gazooka*. This is as much a triumph of creative nonfiction as it is an historically informed novella. The adventure is maniacal, it is hilarious, at times it is moving and tender. We are left in no doubt that in that moment of extraordinary adversity, valleys people found a way to survive, to stare into the face of darkness and to answer back. The camaraderie, the competition, the dressing up, the popular evocation of music and the cinematic imagination, all served to avert wider social anger and so 'to diminish the natural need of frustrated people for some violent expression of their impatience.' As Gwyn put it, movingly, in a final piece to camera:

> We were longing at the beginning of that summer for something that would galvanize life with a new and outrageous happiness because the alternatives, of course, were very dour indeed.

DARYL LEEWORTHY

Daryl Leeworthy was born in Weston-Super-Mare in 1986 but grew up in Ynysybwl near Pontypridd. He studied Modern History and Politics at Oxford and undertook graduate study in Canada. Returning home, he obtained his doctorate from Swansea University and then a series of part-time lecturing jobs including at the University of Huddersfield. He was awarded the Rhys Davies Trust Research Fellowship in 2020 and has since been conferred an honorary research fellowship by Bangor University. He has written extensively across several genres including history, literature, and biography, and his many books include *Labour Country* (2018) and *Fury of Past Time* (2022), the standard life of Gwyn Thomas.

GAZOOKA

GWYN THOMAS

Somewhere outside my window a child is whistling. He is walking fast down the hill and whistling. The tune on his lips is 'Swanee'. I go to the window and watch him. He is moving through a fan of light from a street lamp. His head is thrown back, his lips protrude strongly and his body moves briskly. 'D-I-X-I-Even Mamee, How I love you, how I love you, my dear old Swanee...' The Mississippi and the Taff kiss with dark humming lubricity under an ashen hood of years. Swanee, my dear old Swanee.

The sound of it promotes a roaring life inside my ears. Whenever I hear it, brave ghosts, in endless procession, march again. My eyes are full of the wonder they knew in the months of that long, idle, beautifully lit summer of 1926.

By the beginning of June the hills were bulging with a clearer loveliness than they had ever known before. No smoke rose from the great chimneys to write messages on the sky that puzzled and saddened the minds of the young. The endless journeys of coal trams on the incline, loaded on the upward run, empty and terrifyingly fast on the down, ceased to rattle through the night and mark our dreams. The parade of nailed boots on the pavements at dawn fell silent. Day after glorious day came up over the hills that had been restored by a quirk of social conflict to the calm they lost a hundred years before.

When the school holidays came we took to the mountain tops, joining the liberated pit ponies among the ferns on the broad plateaux. That was the picture for us who were young. For our fathers and mothers there was the inclosing fence of hinted fears, fear of hunger, fear of defeat.

And then, out of the quietness and the golden light, partly to ease their fret, a new excitement was born. The carnivals and the jazz bands.

Rapture can sprout in the oddest places and it certainly sprouted then and there. We formed bands by the dozen, great lumps of beauty and precision, a hundred men and more in each, blowing out their songs as they marched up and down the valleys, amazing and deafening us all. Their instruments were gazookas, with a thunderous bringing up of drums in the rear. Gazookas: small tin zeppelins through which you hummed the tune as loudly as possible. Each band was done up in the uniform of some remote character never before seen in Meadow Prospect. Foreign Legionaries, Chinamen, Carabinieri, Grenadiers, Gauchos, Sultans, Pearl Divers, or what we thought these performers looked like, and there were some very myopic voters among the designers. There was even one group of lads living up on the colder slopes of Mynydd Goch, and eager to put in a word from the world's freezing fringes who did themselves up as Eskimos, but they were liquidated because even Mathew Sewell the Sotto, our leading maestro and musical adviser, could not think up a suitable theme song for boys dressed up as delegates from the Arctic and chronically out of touch with the carnival spirit.

And with the bands came the fierce disputes inseparable from any attempt to promote a little beauty on this planet, the too hasty crowding of chilled men around its small precious flame. The thinkers of Meadow Prospect, a harassed and anxious fringe, gathered in the Discussion Group at the Library and Institute to consider this new marvel. Around the wall was a mural frieze showing a long series of clasped hands staring eyes, symbolising unity and enlightenment among such people as might be expected to turn up in such a room. The chairman was Gomer Gough, known for his addiction to chairmanship as Gough the Gavel. He was broad, wise, enduring and tolerant as our own slashed slopes. He sat at his table underneath two pictures, one a photograph of Tolstoi, a great shaggy lump of sadness, and the other an impression done in charcoal and a brooding spirit, of the betrayal and death of Llewellyn the Last, and as Gomer Gough had often pointed out, it was clear from this drawing that Llewellyn had never had much of a chance.

It was on a Tuesday evening that Milton Nicholas took my Uncle Edwin and myself down to the emergency meeting of the Discussion Group. As we walked down the bare corridor of the Institute we could hear the rustle of bodies and the sough of voices from the Discussion Room. We were solemnly greeted by two very earnest ushers who stood by the door week in, week out, whether they were needed there or no. They had heard so many hot, apocalyptic utterances from the Group they just felt it would be wiser to stay near the door.

'Here, Edwin,' said Milton; 'and you, Iolo, here in the second row.'

'Stop pulling at me, Milton,' said Uncle Edwin. 'Why so far down?'

'This is the place to catch Gomer Gough's eye for a quick question. Gough's eye will have to be very alert tonight.'

'What is this crisis, anyway? Show me the agenda, boy. I don't want to be mixed up in anything frivolous.'

'You know me, Edwin. Always earnest. Uriah Smayle, that neurotic anti-humanist from Cadwallader Crescent, has prepared a very bitter report on the carnivals and bands. Uriah reckons the bands are spreading a mood of pagan laxity among the people and he's out to stop it. I've heard you put up some good lines of argument against Uriah in the past, so just tell your mind to gird up its loins and prepare for its sternest fight. He's a very restrictive element, that Smayle. Any stirring on the face of life and he faints.'

'He's dead against delight, and no doubt at all about it.'

'All right, boy. I'll do what I can. Oh, this is a fine gathering, a room full of people, keen, with their minds out like swords to carve their name on the truth.'

'If that article ever gets as far as this on its travels.'

A man of about forty, ravelled by wariness and rage, looking as sad as Tolstoi but shorter and with no beard and a blue suit, came to sit in the vacant seat just in front of us. He gave us no glance, no greeting.

'Hullo, Uriah,' said Uncle Edwin.

'Good evening,' said Uriah Smayle.

'You're looking very grey and tense tonight, Uriah,' said

Uncle Edwin. 'What new terror is gnawing at you now? If life's a rat, boy, you're the cheese.'

'Well put,' said Milton. 'I've always said that if anybody's got the gift of laying on words like a poultice it's Edwin Pugh the Pang.'

'Mock on, Edwin,' said Uriah, half rising in his seat, his arm up at angle of condemnation. 'But some of my statements tonight are going to shake you rodneys.'

'Good,' said Uncle Edwin. 'Set the wind among our branches, Uriah, and we'll make you a bonus of all the acorns that fall.' His voice was soft and affectionate and he had his hand on Uriah's arm. He was known as Pugh the Pang because he operated as an exposed compassionate nerve on behalf of the whole species. We could see Uriah's spirit sliding down from its plane of high indignation. But he shook himself free from Edwin's arm and got back to form.

'Who's the chairman here?' he asked. 'I've got a meeting of the Young Men's Guild to address at eight on prayer as an answer to lust and it'll be a real relief to have a headful of quiet piety after the chatter of this unbelieving brood.'

'I'm in the chair, Mr Smayle,' said Gomer Gough, who had just walked in followed by Teilo Dew the Doom, our secretary, who had early come under the influence of Carlyle and very tight velveteen trousers. Gomer paused gravely in front of Uriah before turning to take his seat under the face of Tolstoi. 'I'm in the chair, Mr Smayle,' he repeated, 'and I don't rush things. This Discussion Group is out to examine the nature of mankind and the destination of this clinker, the earth.'

Teilo Dew raised his head and winked at Tolstoi and Llewellyn the Last, very sadly, as if suggesting that if he had been a less gentle man he would have told us the black and terrifying answer years ago.

'These are big themes, Mr Smayle,' went on Gomer, 'and we favour a cautious approach. We try not to be hysterical about them, and the best thing you can do is to set a dish of hot leek soup in front of your paler fears.'

'Stop putting yourself to sleep, Gomer,' said Uriah, 'and get on with it.'

Gomer raised his enormous baritone voice like a fist. 'All right,' he said. 'Brothers, at this extraordinary meeting of the Meadow Prospect Discussion Group we are going to hear a special statement from Brother Smayle. He thinks the epidemic of carnivals and costumed bands is a menace and likely to put morals through the mincer. And he says that we, serious thinkers, ought to do something about it.'

'Mr Chairman,' said Uncle Edwin, 'I want you to ask Smayle to tighten his dialectical washers and define this mincer. Tell him, too, that there never has been any period when the morals of mankind, through fear, poverty, ignorance and the rest of the dreary old circus, have not been well minced and ready for the pastry case.'

'Begging your pardon, Edwin,' said Gomer, 'just keep it simmering on the hob, if you don't mind, until Uriah has had his canter. Carry on, Mr Smayle.'

'Mr Chairman,' said Uriah, but he had his body turned and he was speaking straight at Edwin and Milton

Nicholas. 'Since these bands came decency has gone to the dogs. There is something about the sound of a drum that makes the average voter as brazen as a gong. The girls go up in droves to the hillsides where the bands practise, and there is a quality about these gazookas that makes the bandsmen so daring and thoughtless you've got to dig if you want to find modesty any more. Acres of fernland on the plateau to the west left blackened and flat by the scorch stain of depravity.'

Uriah rocked a little and we allowed him a minute to recover from the hubbub created in his mind by that last image. 'And as for the costumes worn by these turnouts, they make me blink. I am thinking particularly of the band led by that Powderhall runner there, Cynlais Coleman the Comet, who is sitting in the fourth row looking very blank and innocent as he always does but no doubt full of mischief.'

We turned around to greet Cynlais Coleman, whom we had not seen until that moment. He was craning forward to hear the whole of Uriah's statement, looking lean, luminous and virgin of guile. Cynlais had aroused wrath in Uriah during his active years as a foot-runner shooting through the streets of Meadow Prospect on trial runs in very short knickers. After he had given us a wide smile of friendliness he returned to looking astounded at what Uriah had just said.

'Who, me?' he asked.

'Yes, you.'

There was a rap from Gomer's gavel and Uriah addressed the chair once more.

'I've always known Cynlais to be as dull as a bat. How does he come to be playing the cuckoo in this nest of thinkers, Gomer? What sinister new alliance is this, boy?'

'Keep personalities out of this, Mr Smayle,' said Gomer.

'Do you mind if I ask Cynlais a few questions about his band?' said Uriah. 'Mr Ephraim Humphries, the ironmonger, has been requested by some of us to serve as moral adviser at large to the carnival committees of the area and he wants me to prepare a special casebook on Cynlais Coleman.'

'Do you mind being questioned, Cynlais?' asked Gomer in his judge's voice.

'Oh no,' said Cynlais. 'You know me, Gomer. Very frank and always keen to help voters like Mr Smayle who are out to keep life scoured and fresh to the smell.'

A lot of voices around Cynlais applauded his willingness to undergo torment by Uriah's torch.

'Now tell me, Cynlais, my boy,' began Uriah. 'I have now watched you in three carnivals, and each time you've put me down for the count with worry and shock. Let me explain why, Mr Chairman. He marches at the head of a hundred young elements, all of them half naked, with little more than the legal minimum covered over with bits of old sheet, and Cynlais himself working up a colossal gleam of frenzy in his eye. He does a short sprint at Powderhall speed and then returns to the head of his retinue looking as if he's just gone off the hinge that very morning. Cynlais is no better dressed than his followers. His bits of sheet are thicker and whiter but they hang even looser about the body. He also has a way, when on the march, of giving his body a violent jerk which makes him look even more demented. This is popular among the thoughtless, and I have heard terrible shrieks of approval from some who are always present at these morally loose-limbed events. But I warn Cynlais that one day he will grossly overdo those pagan leaps and find his feet a good yard to the north of his loin cloth, and a frost on his torso that will finish him for such events as the Powderhall Dash, and even for the commonplace carnality that has been his main hobby to date. His band also plays "Colonel Bogey", an ominous tune even when played by the Meadow Prospect Silver Jubilee Band in full regalia. But Coleman's boys play it at slow march tempo as if to squeeze the last drop of significance out of it. Now tell me, Coleman, what's the meaning of all this? What lies behind these antics, boy? What are you supposed to be, and I ask with a real fear of being answered.'

'Dervishes,' said Cynlais Coleman. 'We are dervishes, Mr Smayle.'

'Dervishes? What are they?'

'A kind of fanatic. We got the idea from Edwin Pugh the Pang there. When we told him that we were very short of fabric for our costumes and that we'd got no objection to going around looking shameless, out he came with this suggestion that we should put on a crazed, bare, prophetic look, as if we'd just come in from the desert with an old sunstroke and a fresh revelation.'

Uriah was now nodding his head and looking horrified as if his finger, eroded and anguished by a life's inquiry, had now found and fondled the central clod from which all the darkness of malignity flowered.

'You've been the tool of some terrible plotters, Cynlais. And is that leap to show that you are now shaking the sand out of your sash?'

'Oh no. I'm not worried about the sand at all, Mr Smayle. This leap in the air is just to show that I am the leader of these Dervishes, the Mad Mahdi. I got a lot of information about him from that very wise voter who never shifts from the Reading Room downstairs, Jedediah Knight the Light.'

'I'm here,' said a voice from the back. It was Jedediah Knight, resting his eyes in the shadows of the back row and looking, as he always did, shocked by understanding and wearied by the search for things that merit the tribute of being understood. 'But I told him that the Mahdi would never have advanced against the Empire playing so daring a tune and with so little on.'

'What do you say to these charges, Cynlais?' asked Gomer.

'Fair enough, Gomer,' said Cynlais. 'When we get enough money for new costumes we'll come in out of the Middle East at a fast trot.'

'Any more, Mr Smayle?' asked Gomer.

'A lot more. I have a pint of gall on my mind about that woman's band organised by Georgie Young but that will have to wait.'

He made for the door with long, urgent strides and the two ushers fell back.

'Goodnight,' we all shouted, but the sound that came back from Uriah was just a blur.

'Come on, Edwin,' said Milton Nicholas. 'Let's go and have some tea and beef extract at Tasso's.'

Later that night, at Paolo Tasso's Coffee Tavern, my Uncle Edwin was a lot less serene than usual. Over a glass of scalding burdock, which he drank because someone had told him it made a man callous and jocose, he admitted that he'd been thinking a lot about what Uriah Smayle had said. He made it clear to us that he was in no way siding with Uriah. The pageantry of life had long passed us by in Meadow Prospect and he was glad of the colour and variety brought into our streets by the costumes worn by some of the boys. It would help us, he said, to recover from the sharp clip behind the ear dealt us by the Industrial Revolution. But all the same, he claimed, he could see dangers in this eruption of Mediterranean flippancy and joy.

'We have worn ourselves over the years bald and handy trying to bring a little thought and uplift to this section of the fringe. Not even a Japanese shirt shrinks more swiftly than awareness. It's been cold, lonely work trying to push the ape back into the closet. Now with all these drum beats and marching songs the place could well become a mental boneyard overnight.'

There was such a plangent tolling in his voice that the steam ceased to rise from his burdock and Tasso offered to warm it for him again, but Uncle Edwin said that at that moment a stoup of cold cordial was just the thing for him.

But few of us agreed with Uncle Edwin. For all the young a tide of delight flowed in with the carnivals. At first we had two bands in Meadow Prospect; Cynlais Coleman's Dervishes and the Boys from Dixie. The Boys from Dixie wore black suits and we never got to know where voters with so little surplus to buy bottles ever got the cork from to make themselves look so dark. They were good marchers, though, and it was impressive to see these one hundred and twenty jet-black pillars moving down the street in perfect formation playing 'Swanee' in three lines of harmony.

There were some who said it was typical of a gloomy place like Meadow Prospect that it should have one band walking about in no tint save sable and looking like an instalment of eternal night, while another, Cynlais Coleman's, left you wondering whether to give it a good clap or a strong strait-jacket. But we took some pride from the fact that at marching the Boys from Dixie could not be beaten. Their driller and coach was a cantankerous and aged imperialist called Georgie Young the Further Flung, a solitary and chronic dissenter from Meadow Prospect's general radicalism. Georgie had fought in several of our African wars and Uncle Edwin said it gave Georgie some part of his youth back to have this phalanx of darkened elements wheeling and turning every whipstitch at his shout of command.

Most of the bands went in for vivid colours, though a century of chapel-bound caution had left far too little coloured fabric to go around. If any voter had any showy stuff at home he was well advised to sit tight on the box, or the envoy of some band would soon be trundling off with every stitch of it to succour some colleagues who had been losing points for his band by turning out a few inches short in the leg or deficient in one sleeve. We urged Georgie Young that the Boys from Dixie should brighten themselves up a little, with a yellow sash or even a scarlet fez, a tight-fitting and easily made article which gave a very dashing look to the Tredomen Janissaries, a Turkish body. But Georgie was obdurate. His phobias were down in a lush meadow and grazing hard. It was black from tip to toe or nothing, he said. However, he relented somewhat when he formed the first women's band. These were a broad-bodied, vigorous crew, strong on charabanc outings that finished on a note of blazing revelry with these elements drinking direct from the petrol tank. Their band had uniforms made roughly of the colour and pattern of the national flag. The tune they played on their gazookas was 'Rule, Britannia'. They began well every time they turned out, but they were invariably driven off-key by their shyer members who could not keep their minds on the score of 'Rule, Britannia' while their Union Jacks kept slipping south with the convulsive movements of quick marching on sudden slopes. They had even called in Mathew Sewell the Sotto as musical adviser and Mathew had given them a grounding in self-confidence and sol-fa. But they went as out of tune as ever. Jedediah Knight the Light, fresh from a short brush with Einstein, said that if they got any worse they would surely reach the bend in musical space which would bring them willy-nilly back to the key first given them by Sewell the Sotto on his little tuning fork. Nevertheless, both of Georgie's bands, the dour Boys from Dixie and the erratic Britannias, had a smartness that completely eclipsed Cynlais Coleman's bedraggled covey in their flapping fragments of sheet.

So it was decided by the group that met at Tasso's that the time had come to arrange a new deal for the Dervishes. It was agreed that they were altogether too inscrutable for an area so in need of new and clear images.

It was left to Mathew Sewell, who knew more about the bands than anybody else and had operated as a judge in half a dozen smaller carnivals, to put the matter to Cynlais.

Cynlais came along to Tasso's one Thursday night for a talk with his critics. It was still July but Tasso had his big stove on full in the middle of the shop because he had a group of older clients who had never been properly warm since the flood of 1911. Tea all round was ordered and Mathew Sewell stood in the middle of the room, with his hand up, ready to start, but he had to wait a few minutes for the hissing of the tea urn and the rattling of teacups to abate. As a specialist in the head voice, he hated to speak in a shout.

After a sip of tea Sewell summarised for the benefit of those who were new to this issue of Cynlais' band the findings of Smayle and the other censors. Then he addressed Cynlais directly:

'So you see, Cynlais, there are no two twos about it.

You've got to put a stop to this business of going about half nude. It's out of place in such a division as this. I speak as an artist and without malice. But it's about time you and the boys dressed in something a bit more tasteful. Something soft and sensuous, that's what we want.'

Cynlais drank his tea while Uncle Edwin stroked the back of his head, encouraging him to be lucid. Then Cynlais put up his hand to show Edwin that the message had worked and he said:

'I say to you, Mathew, what I said to Uriah Smayle and Ogley Floyd the Flame and those other very fierce elements. Get us the costumes and we'll all be as soft and sensuous as you like. Like cream.'

'That's the spirit,' said Mathew. 'Think it over now, and when you're fitted out consult me about the music and I'll prescribe some tune with a lullaby flavour that you can march to.' Mathew threw such hints of the soporific into the word 'lullaby' that some of the people in Tasso's looked disturbed, as if afraid that if Sewell were given a free wand Cynlais' hand would be the first in the area to wind up asleep on the kerb halfway through the carnival. Mathew saw their expression and, always averse to argument, said: 'I've got to go now. *Bono notte*, Signor Tasso.'

'So long, Mathew,' we all said, feeling a certain shabbiness on our tongues. Cynlais was staring at the door that had just shut behind Mathew.

'Did you hear that?' asked Cynlais. 'Oh he's so smooth and operatic, that Sewell the Sotto. A treat.' He turned to Tasso, who was leaning over the counter in his long white shop coat, his toffee hammer sticking out of the breast pocket, his face grey, joyless but unwaveringly sympathetic. 'Don't you like to have Sewell come out with these little bits of Italian, Tasso?'

'It is true, Cynlais,' said Tasso. 'More than once Signor Sewell the Sotto has eased the burden of my old longing for Lugano.'

Gomer Gough the Gavel got order once again by tapping with his cup on the cast-iron fireguard.

'Now let's get down to this,' said Gomer. 'We've got to fit Cynlais up with a band that will make a contribution to beauty and keep Uriah Smayle out of the County Clinic. We can't leave the field undisputed to Georgie Young and his Boer War fancies.' There was a silence for a minute. Hard thought scoured the inside of every head bent towards the stove as history was raked for character and costume suitable for Cynlais and his followers. Tasso tapped on the counter with his toffee hammer to keep the meditation in rhythm. Then Gomer looked relieved as if he had just stepped in from a high wind. We all smiled to welcome his revelation but we stopped smiling when he said:

'Have you got any money, Cynlais?'

'Money? Money?' said Cynlais and our eyebrows backed him up because we thought Gomer Gough's question pointless at that point in our epoch.

'Forget that I asked,' said Gomer. 'But I think it's a shame that a boy like you who made so much at the coal face and at professional running should now be whittled down to a loincloth for the summer and a double-breasted waistcoat for the winter.' Gomer's eyes wandered around the room until they landed on Milton Nicholas. 'Come here, Milton. You've been looking very nimble-witted since you were voted on to the Library committee. How do you think Cynlais Coleman could get hold of some money to deck out his band in something special? I mean some way that won't have Cynlais playing his last tune through the bars of the County Keep.'

'Well, he's still known as Coleman the Comet for his speed off the mark. Wasn't it Paavo Nurmi, the great Finn, who once said that it wouldn't surprise him if Cynlais Coleman turned out to be the only athlete ever to be operated on for rockets in the rear?' We all nodded yes but felt that Milton had probably never heard of this Nurmi until that morning and was only slipping in the name to make a striking effect. Gomer urged Milton to forget the Finn and get back to the present. 'Let him find somebody who wants to hire a fast runner,' added Milton.

'In this area at the moment, Milton, even an antelope would have to make Welsh cakes and mint toffee on the side to make both ends meet. Be practical, boy.'

'I'm being practical. I heard today that a group of sporting elements in Trecelyn with a definite bias against serious thought are going to stage a professional sprint with big cash prizes. Comes off in three weeks.'

'Don't forget that Cynlais is getting on a bit,' said Teilo Dew, 'for this high-class running anyway. I've heard him wheeze a bit on the sharper slopes.'

'Trust Teilo Dew the Doom to chip in with an item like that,' said Milton bitterly. 'Whenever Teilo talks to you he's peering at you from between his two old friends, Change and Decay. In three weeks Cynlais could be at his best and if you boys could take up a few collections to lay bets on him we'd have a treasury.'

'That's a very backward habit, gambling,' said Uncle Edwin.

'Remind me to hire a small grave for the scruples of Edwin Pugh the Pang,' said Gomer. 'Right. That's how we'll raise the cash. Off to bed with you now, Cynlais. You've got to be as fit as a fiddle for the supreme test. No more staying up till twelve and drinking hot cordial in Tasso's.'

Cynlais had heard very little of all this. He had been staring into the fire and pondering on what Mathew Sewell had said. He was shocked when he suddenly found supporters coming from all over the shop and helping him to his feet and leading him with half a dozen lines of advice at the same time.

'Don't sleep crouched, Coleman; it obstructs the pipes.'

'Keep even your dreams chaste, Cynlais; if the libido played hell with Samson, what mightn't it do to you?'

'An hour's sleep before midnight is worth two after.'

'Slip Coleman some of those brown lozenges, Tasso, the ones that deepen the breathing.'

'A foot race is a kind of battle, Cynlais. Make a plan for every foot.'

Then Teilo Dew the Doom waved them all to silence and started to tell Cynlais about some very noted foot runner in the zone who had raced and died about two hundred years ago after outpacing all the fleeter animals and breaking every record. Everybody was glad to hear Teilo Dew opening out on what for him was a comparatively blithe topic but expressions went back to normal when Teilo reached the climax of his tale. At the end of this man's last race his young bride had clapped him on the back and the runner had dropped down dead.

'I know that you are not married, Cynlais,' said Teilo, 'and that you have few relatives who would want to watch you run or do anything else, but there are several voters in Meadow Prospect who would find real relish in hanging around the finishing tape and giving you a congratulatory whack just in the hope of sending you lifeless to the ground.'

Cynlais shook himself free from his supporters and was going to ask the meaning of all this fuss but Tasso just raised his toffee hammer solemnly, which is what he always did when he wished to say that he, too, was foxed.

We all joined in the task of helping Cynlais regain his old tremendous speed. We got him training every night up on the waun, the broad, bleak, wind filled moorland above the town. Sometimes Cynlais was like a stag, and our only trouble was to keep up with him and give him tips and instructions and fit his neck back when he went flying over molehills. At first he was a bit stiff around the edges owing to a touch of rheumatism from standing in too many High Street breezes in the role of dervish. Milton Nicholas got some wheel-grease from the gasworks, where he was a leading fitter, and Uncle Edwin, whose sympathy of soul made his fingers just the thing for slow massage, rubbed this stuff into Cynlais until both he and Cynlais got so supple they had to be held upright for minutes on end.

We looked after Cynlais' nourishment, too, for his diet had been scraggy over the last few months. Teilo Dew approached that very sullen farmer Nathan Wilkins up on the top of the hill we called Merlin's Brow, and asked him for some goat milk. Wilkins took pleasure in saying no loudly for as long as Dew was within earshot, and even the goat was seen to shake its head from side to side. So Teilo bypassed Nathan Wilkins and approached the goat direct, and in no time we had Cynlais growing stronger daily. But there was still something jerky and unpredictable in some of his movements. So Gomer Gough and Uncle Edwin decided to consult their friend Willie Silcox. He was called Silcox the Psyche because he was the greatest tracker in our valley of those nameless beasts that roam our inward jungles. If Silcox saw anyone with a look of even slight perplexity on his face he would be out with the guidebook and fanning them with Freud before they could start running. He had analysed so many people into a state of dangerous confusion that the town's joint diaconate had advised him to go back to simple religious mania as being a lot safer and easier on the eyes because you could work up to full heat without reading a word. Silcox had just told the joint diaconate that he was watching them closely and making notes.

A week before the race at Trecelyn we met Willie Silcox at Tasso's. Silcox was leaning over the counter and we all saw as we came in that he had never looked or felt more penetrating. Tasso, who was all for indirection and compromise as the right climate for the catering trade, had shifted away from Silcox and was standing very close to the urn. People claiming to be forthrightly wise frightened the wits out of Tasso. At the sight of us Silcox waved us to stillness while he finished off a quick note he was giving Tasso on what he thought the joint effects of exile and the cash nexus would be on a middle-aged Italian. Tasso said nothing but put his head right against the urn for greater comfort.

'Have a beef extract with us, Willie,' said Gomer. 'Glad you were able to come, boy.'

'Thank you, Gomer. What mental stoppage have you got for me to disperse now?'

'Oh I'm all right. My pipes were never more open. It's Cynlais Coleman I'm worried about.'

'Look, Gomer. Before we go any further, let me make this clear. To prescribe a pill for the mentally ill the patient must have a mind. That's in the rule book and that's the first smoke signal I would like you to send out to Coleman. That element, mentally, is still unborn. What makings of a mind he might still have had he not dropped into the bin years ago by trying to outrun the wind, and setting up as a great lover in an area that favours a slow humility in affairs of the heart.'

'Don't quibble, Willie. Cynlais isn't running as well as he should and we want the cure.'

'All right. Take me to where I can see him and if I can find a pole long enough to reach the end of Coleman's furthest cranny I'll give you a report and charge you for the pole because I'll never get it back after a journey like that.'

The next night we went with Willie Silcox up to the waun. Cynlais and a group of supporters were already there and Cynlais was finishing a trial sprint. We could hear as we approached shouts like: 'Come on, Cynlais.' 'Let's have you Coleman.' 'Don't look around, boy.' 'Show us your real paces, Comet.'

Then we heard Cynlais run headlong into the group around the tape, sending several of them spinning, and we could see that he himself was lurching and gasping painfully. 'Well done,' said Uncle Edwin without conviction.

Cynlais was making noises like a pump, and writhing. Milton Nicholas was standing over Cynlais and looking as if the campaign had reached some sort of crisis.

'Put your head between your legs and squeeze hard, Cynlais boy. That'll cool you off.'

Cynlais tried to do this and went into a brief convulsion. Several voters told Milton Nicholas to mind his own business, which was gas fitting. And there were a few very shrewd elements in the group who said they would not be surprised to find that Milton Nicholas had laid a week's wages on all the other runners but Cynlais in that race at Trecelyn.

'The aim of Nicholas,' I heard one of them say, 'is to get Coleman into a knot and let him choke.'

Gomer Gough turned to Willie Silcox, who had not taken his eyes off Cynlais.

'Well, Willie. What's your diagnosis?'

'Easy,' said Willie, and from the offhand, flippant way in which he said it we thought he was going to suggest that Cynlais be saddled in harness with Wilkins' goat and told to forget about foot-racing. 'Easy. Do you notice the way he seems to pause sometimes in his running and look back?'

'He does it all the time,' said Uncle Edwin. 'He hardly ever looks straight in front.'

'That's a habit he got into while acting as the Mad Mahdi. All fanatics are persecution maniacs and anybody who introduces Mahometan overtones into the Celtic fringe was bound to hit some kind of top note. Cynlais has now got into the way of looking over his shoulder even in the middle of the waun where his shoulder is about the only thing in sight. And again, that band of Cynlais' contains some torpid boys even for gazooka players, and Cynlais is so fleet he has to keep turning to make sure that he and they are still in the same town. But Coleman's real trouble is love.'

'Love?' asked Gomer Gough and Uncle Edwin and it was clear from their tone that they were now both sorry that they had brought Silcox up the mountain at all.

'Love,' repeated Willie Silcox in exactly the voice of a sanitary inspector making a report to the borough surveyor.

'But Cynlais told me only two days ago that he was no longer worried about this impulse.'

'I've only got to look at a man and I can sniff the urge to love and be loved, however deep and quiet it flows. For months Cynlais has been hopelessly in love with that girl, Moira Hallam.'

'Moira Hallam? That dark, blazing-eyed girl from Sebastopol Street?'

'That's the one. The thoughts that that girl inspires in a single day would fill a whole shelf in the Institute and you'd need a strong binding to keep them in the case.'

'And she's turned Cynlais down?'

'She looks at him with disgust and treats him with contempt.'

'But wouldn't this make Cynlais run even better, to show off?'

'You don't know, Gomer, what a cantankerous article the mind is. Even as he runs Cynlais looks down at the fine, big chest under his singlet and becomes aware of his frustrated passions. It's a wall, a cruel blank wall. His heart breaks his nose against it. His limbs wince and they lose pace.'

'Willie,' said Gomer, 'I can never listen to you without feeling that you put a new and terrible complexion on this planet.'

'Anything to oblige. And let me warn you about this Moira Hallam. She is an imperialist of the flesh, very ruthless. You know that old widower, Alfie Cranwell. He had money saved to provide the deposit on a headstone for the grave of his deceased wives. Blew the lot on a watch for this Moira Hallam. But he would have found the headstone softer. She works in that cake shop they call the Cosmo. Cranwell kept hanging about the shop nipping in and wolfing cakes despite strong warnings about sugar from his doctor. Died of a surfeit. All this Moira did was boast about the bonus she had from the manageress of the Cosmo on the brisk selling she had done to Cranwell in the last weeks of his passion.'

Gomer and Uncle Edwin tut-tutted as if this girl was just another in a long series of obstructions they had found giving life a dark and strangled look.

'Well, thank you, Willie. We'll bear your report in mind.'

But Willie Silcox was not listening. He was staring past Gomer at some member of the group around Cynlais, beneath the apparently bland surface of whose days Willie's dowser had sensed some concealed runnel of trouble. This man was smiling quite broadly at something Milton Nicholas had just said and he did not know how lucky he still was with Willie Silcox standing at a safe distance from him.

Later that evening I was walking along the main street of Meadow Prospect with my Uncle Edwin, helping him to make a casual check on the number of people who seemed to be at ease on the earth. The first person we found who really seemed to be so was Gomer Gough the Gavel, and before Edwin could tell Gomer about this Gomer was hurrying the both of us down a side street.

'Where to now, Gomer?' asked Uncle Edwin tartly.

'Moira Hallam's.'

'What for?'

'To talk her out of this nonsense of frustrating and slowing down Cynlais Coleman the Comet. You heard what Willie Silcox said. Between being a dervish and a disappointed lover, it's a wonder Cynlais can walk, let alone run at his old Powderhall lick.'

'Oh leave me out of this, Gomer. Here were Iolo and I, on a serious social beat, staring at the voters and trying to estimate how many mental inches separated them from the County Clinic. Leave us be. I'm not interested in Cynlais anymore and I don't know this Moira Hallam, except to feel vaguely grateful to her for having helped to shuffle off Alfie Cranwell, who was, as a ram, indiscriminate, irrational and a nuisance.'

'I want you to come along to Moira's house for the very reason that you're called Edwin Pugh the Pang. You are so full of pity the sight and sound of you would bring tears even to the eyes of Nathan Wilkins, the only gorsedd stone ever to opt for hillside farming and working in trousers of heavy corduroy. You can play on the feelings of this Moira. Don't be surprised if, at the door of the Hallam home, I introduce you as Cynlais Coleman's father, who took up thinking instead of sprinting.'

Uncle Edwin was on the point of opening his mouth to tell Gomer Gough to go and jump into the deeper reach of the Moody, our river, when Gomer stopped outside one of a long row of identical houses and said: 'Here we are.'

I was about to move off but he held me back and said he preferred a mixed delegation.

'If we need a statement from the youth of Meadow Prospect, Iolo, to support our own pleas, we'd like to have you on hand. Just turn a possible statement over in your mind while you're waiting.'

The door opened to Gomer's knock. Mrs Hallam, the mother of Moira, was a big, vigorous woman whose eyes and arms gave the impression of being red and steaming.

'Oh good evening to you, Mrs Hallam,' said Gomer, with what he thought was a courtly bow copied from Cunninghame Graham, whom he had once seen at a socialist rally, but Gomer was at least a foot too short to make this gesture look anything but an attempt to duck for safety. Mrs Hallam sprang back into the passage, thinking that Gomer was going to butt her.

'What do you want?' she said. 'If you are after my husband to join that old Discussion Group again you can save your wind. The last time he went the topic was capital punishment and hanging and so forth and he had the migraine for a week. Anything about pressure on the neck and the poor dab is off.'

'No, we are not here about that. It's about your daughter, Moira.'

'All day long there's a knock on the door and it's the same old tale. Moira, Moira, Moira. But you are the two oldest performers to turn up so far, I'll say that. Why don't you two boys stick to debating?'

Uncle Edwin groaned and came to flatten himself against the patch of wall against which I had already flattened myself trying to think out what the youth of

Meadow Prospect might have to say to Mrs Hallam. Uncle Edwin spoke in a dramatic whisper:

'Here am I, my senses in this field of carnality out for the count since 1913, and I have to stand here and listen to this prattle.'

Gomer pulled Edwin back into the field of play.

'We are here, Mrs Hallam, on behalf of that fine runner, Cynlais Coleman.' It was clear from the drop of Mrs Hallam's jaw that she had never heard a sentence she had followed less well.

'What's he running for? Whenever my husband runs he gets the migraine.'

Gomer slipped into his voice the fine bel canto effect he used when he quoted the Bible at public meetings to support social change.

'Mrs Hallam, Cynlais Coleman loves your daughter.'

Uncle Edwin groaned again and I, hoping it might help us to get off that doorstep, groaned with him. There was also a short whimper from beyond the dimly lighted passageway which I took to be Mr Hallam switching on to a fresh track of his endemic migraine. But Gomer went straight on: 'He's losing sleep and health over her, Mrs Hallam. We were wondering if you...'

'Not a hope,' said Mrs Hallam, and she seemed triumphant that after thirty years of indeterminate and depressing interviews at that front door she had at last come across one topic about which she could be utterly final. 'Moira was in the Trecelyn Amateur Operatics last winter. They did Carmen and now she's daft about that baritone Moelwyn Cox, who took the part of the toreador. You ought to see his velvet coat and his satin breeches. So tight, so shiny, a treat.'

Edwin pulled strongly at Gomer's coat.

'Gomer,' he said, very softly, 'could I make a short statement here that would cover both love and bull-fighting?'

'No,' said Gomer, so quietly Mrs Hallam thrust her head forward to keep a check on what was going on. 'Sebastopol Street is no place to be discussing ethics. You know that, boy.' He raised his voice and then said to Mrs Hallam in a voice that came as close to the bedside manner as Gomer would ever get on the street side of the front door: 'Mrs Hallam, how is your husband's migraine now?'

Mrs Hallam looked at Gomer suspiciously. She was probably marshalling in her mind memories of some of the gloomy specifics for mankind's many ails which had been recommended at the Discussion Group of which her husband had been a transient member.

'Oh, not bad,' she said. 'Twice a week he wears a turban of brown paper soaked in vinegar and it's like having chips in the house. A treat.' She raised her arm and smiled as if wishing to convince Gomer that she regarded this turban motif as the last word, and she wanted no hints from him or Uncle Edwin.

'Will you put in a word with Moira for Cynlais Coleman?'

'I'll mention it. But only because you asked about the migraine. Sympathy is what matters. But I can tell you now, Moira is daft about Moelwyn Cox.'

We made our way back down the street. Darkness had fallen. Our steps were loud and had a flavour. Gomer Gough was staring at the great-looking shape of Merlin's Crown. Uncle Edwin was shaking his head in desperation and warning me in general terms not to get mixed up in anything, not with Gomer Gough or Silcox as a partner anyway.

On the day of the Trecelyn Sports a large body of us left Meadow Prospect to see Cynlais run. There was a huge crowd and the sports field, converted by the flimsiest manoeuvres from being an ordinary field, was full, well-flagged and happy. Cynlais was right in the middle of us and he had been on edge during that walk to Trecelyn by having Uncle Edwin sidling up to him on the pavement and giving him a little supplementary massage.

'Stop doing that, for God's sake, Edwin. You never know what people will think.'

He broke away from us as we entered the field, glad, for a few seconds, to be rid of us.

'How do you think Cynlais is feeling, Gomer?' asked Uncle Edwin.

'Fine, Edwin. Can't you see he looks fine?'

'Frankly, I think there is a very lax, bemused look about him. He doesn't seem too solid on his pins to me. Milton Nicholas says he's been over trained and worn down to the canvas by having to dodge those molehills up on the waun while travelling faster than light, and making sense of the axioms of Willie Silcox the Psyche while travelling mentally not at all.' Uncle Edwin thrust his lips out to show that he was sick and tired of giving consideration to Cynlais. Then his face lit up. 'They've certainly enjoyed full employment, those moles up on the waun. What the hell is their motive in shifting all that earth?'

Milton Nicholas, a nature lover, was going to explain when Gomer Gough broke in roughly:

'Don't go saying things like that to Cynlais. The race is due in twenty minutes and I don't want to upset him. For temperament he's worse than any tenor. I told him that Mrs Hallam was going to do all she could for him. That'll buck him up a bit. But I'm taking no chances. You know how upset he was last Monday?'

'Last Monday?' Edwin for a week had been busy preparing a monograph for the Discussion Group proving that the Celt must at one time have been half drowned in ale and half crazed by lust to have been so busy scalping the drink trade and the flesh ever since.

'What happened last Monday?'

'Cynlais' band and the Boys from Dixie went to the carnival at Tregysgod and Georgie Young didn't finish last only because Cynlais was there before him. It's enough to drive Matthew Sewell the Sotto off his head notes. Cynlais' band lost points for obscurity and brazen indecency, so the judges said, and Georgie's platoon was denounced as too sombre, too austere. It was a terrible day for Meadow Prospect. So I went to Kitchener Caney.'

We drew closer. We were all astonished. Caney was a whimsical mixer of simples, a most inaccurate herbalist and healer.

'Caney the Cure?' asked Uncle Edwin. 'Caney the Herbs?'

'That's him. Compared with Caney, Merlin was a learner. He was most interested when I told him about Cynlais. He says that slowness and sadness are both great evils and that somewhere in fields is some tiny plant that has the full answer to them both.

'And Caney's the boy to find it. And when he spreads it around there'll be no one around to be sad or slow.

'He gave me a herbal concoction for Cynlais. He made no charge although the bottle he gave me was the largest I've seen containing herbs. It's called "Soul Balm". That's what it says on the label. It makes the heart serene and oblivious and it sounds to like the sort of thing most of the voters ought to be belting at the livelong day.'

'Cynlais is certainly oblivious,' said Edwin. 'Look at him over there now. He looks as dull as a bat.'

'I got Tasso to slip Cynlais the balm in his last cocoa and for the next few hours his mind will be sunlit.'

Cynlais came towards us. He was dejected and he was shooting his limbs perversely in different directions.

'Here he is now,' said Gomer, very cheerfully. 'Just look at him, Edwin. I've seen taller men, wiser men, but fitter and faster, never!'

Cynlais gave us all a plaintive, pleading look. 'I've just seen Moira over there, by that flagpole.'

'I see her. Eyes made to glow like headlamps by some artifice or other and her skirt three inches shorter than it was last week. Is this blatant provocation or is she tucking the thing up for wading?'

'Could I nip over and have a chat with her, Gomer?'

'Not before the race. She's got even the flagpole bending over for a look. Keep your mind on the job in hand and think of the prize money that will get you out of those shameful costumes you wear as dervishes.' Gomer scanned the field. 'I see some very keen-looking athletes here. Boys who pause only to breed and feed. You'll have to stay calm as a rock and sharp as a knife to win the prize against this competition. If you linger for any traffic with that Moira Hallam we'd have to launch you from the starting line on a stretcher and the Trecelyn Silver Band over there would have to switch from "Anchors Aweigh" to that very slow piece from Saul.'

Cynlais took one look at Moira Hallam. It was too much for him. He went bouncing towards her, using the same clownish and ataxic gait as before.

'Come back here, you jay,' shouted Gomer. 'Oh, dammo!'

'Caney the Cure is at work here,' said Uncle Edwin. 'He probably put some ingredient in that mixture that blows every gonad into a flame. In a moment you'll see that Moira Hallam shinning up that flagpole and Coleman will be just one hot breath behind her scorching off the paintwork.'

Gomer took me by the shoulder and told me to stay close to Cynlais and keep reminding him of his duty to Meadow Prospect, and Uncle Edwin gave me a few discouraging things about romantic love to pass on to Cynlais if the chance arose.

Cynlais stood a modest five or six feet from Moira. I stared at Moira, my senses candent and amazed. Her eyes had the searing, purposive lustre of opened furnaces and in the hem of her skirt, almost as far away from the ground as the flag on the pole, a new dimension of arrogance was given to sex. Moira's body and urges were meant to last and it was a relief to turn from her to study the resigned limpness of the flag, from which the starch of a dynamic tribalism had long since been laved.

Cynlais just stood there with a dropped jaw and I had to give him a nudge to remind him that if he did not want Gomer and Milton Nicholas and the other fanciers to be closing in on him and applying violence, the best thing he could do was to deliver some simple message to Moira and marshal his thoughts for a bit of foot-racing. Cynlais pulled his jaw back into position and a beauty of longing settled on his face. In that mood he could have come out with a splurge of words that would have struck a new top note in bedroom rhetoric. But all he said was:

'Hullo, Moira. Oh, it's good to see you again after so long.'

'Don't talk to me, Cynlais Coleman,' said Moira. Her voice was sharply impatient, but even Moira's wrath had an edge of lubricious softness. 'You ought to be ashamed of yourself. First of all jumping about like a madman at the head of that band, half naked and putting the preachers on edge, then sending those two jokers to my front door to get around my mother, indeed. What kind of serpent are you developing into, Cynlais?'

'They didn't tell me they were going, honest. Gomer and Edwin were working off their own bats, and you know what a pair of terrors they are for being deep and unexpected. Can I see you tonight, Moira?'

'Not tonight or ever. I'm meeting Moelwyn Cox in front of the Gaiety at seven. Plush seats, back row, one and three, made to measure. Have you ever seen Moelwyn in his bullfighter's uniform? After that you'll always look very colourless to me, Cynlais. Has your heart ever been in the orange groves of Seville?'

'Never. You know that, Moira. The furthest I've been is that bus trip to Tintern Abbey with the Buffs.' The last word came out like a sort of groaning gasp, as if someone had knocked all the wind out of Cynlais from behind. I thought this a very poor augury for the race and I was on the point of giving Cynlais a monitory kick on the shin when Moira let out a laugh that was so loud, contemptuous and yet passionately stimulant it put her instantly under the same shawl as Carmen. Gomer Gough was making that very point when we got back into earshot of the Meadow Prospect group.

'You hear that laugh?' Gomer was asking. 'The sight of Moelwyn Cox's satin breeches has got that girl into a state where she could give a night-school course on lust as a tactic. Come on, Cynlais. Forget about Seville and get your knicks on. The only answer to Moelwyn Cox showing his cloak to the bull is you showing your butts to all humanity by leading the field here today.'

'I don't go all the way with Nietzsche,' said Uncle

Edwin, 'but the only recipe is the brutal force of triumph for that sort of girl.'

Cynlais looked puzzled by that statement and Gomer had to explain. Then Cynlais looked downcast again.

'I couldn't look at my knicks today, Gomer, not after that. I haven't got the heart. Not after that.'

'Come on,' said Milton Nicholas. 'Think of the prize money.'

'Aye, and the stinging way those judges spoke to you last Monday,' said Gomer. 'One of them said that your band had undone a whole century of progressive work by the Sunday School union. And he said, too, that as soon as they could raise the fare to Africa the whole pack of you would be on the boat addressed to the jungle.'

Uncle Edwin was staring into the further distance and following the movements of a very large man who was clearly an official and wearing the type of multilateral hat worn by Sherlock Holmes, but this hat was in a kind of tweed material and untidier than the hats we have seen on Holmes.

'Look over there,' said Edwin. 'There's that big auctioneer, Erasmus John the Going Gone, wearing a cloth hat and shaking his gun to show that he's the starter.'

'He's a very cunning boy, that Erasmus John,' said Milton, 'and not only at auctions either. I hear he's got a favourite of his own competing here today.' Milton jumped forward and frightened the wits out of the abstracted Cynlais by urgently grasping his sleeve. 'Keep your eye on Erasmus John the Going Gone, Cynlais. Watch that he doesn't confuse you. Politically and morally that man has for thirty years been master of the false alarm. See that he keeps his auctioneering slogans out of the formula used for starting this race.'

'All right then. For your sake that's all. That Moira... Just one look from her and she scoops the heart right out of me, leaving not even the wish to whistle.' Cynlais straightened his back and gave his head a little shake. 'But I've got it in for that Erasmus John. He was one of the judges at Tregysgod last Monday. He came to see us after the judging, sneering and laughing.'

'I was there,' said Milton. 'I heard him and the things he said were a disgrace for a man who's supposed to keep an open mind. He said that he would like to lay Cynlais as a wreath on the grave of General Gordon who was speared to death by dervishes in the unlimited phase of our imperial adventure. He also said, that as a Christian, he was arranging to have the final mark won by Cynlais' band announced direct by muezzin if the Tregysgod council could throw up some sort of rough minaret. You can imagine how all these references foxed Cynlais and the boys and made them feel that they were standing in a chilling draught of contempt and rejection.'

'Hellish things for draughts, those bits of loose sheeting,' said Cynlais. He waved his arm in goodbye and made his way towards the ramshackle pavilion where the athletes were to change.

'Good luck, Cyn,' we all shouted.

'And watch that Erasmus John,' said Milton Nicholas.

'With that length of gun and that style of hat he won't consider today complete until he's shot somebody. Somebody from Meadow Prospect for preference who turns out in carnivals in an overtly anti-British costume. So watch out.'

'I will,' Cynlais shouted back. He tried to make his voice cheerful but we could see that not even his little spurt of rebellion against the insolence of Erasmus John had given him back anything like his usual vim.

'That soul balm of Caney's is wearing off,' said Uncle Edwin.

'Caney should have doubled the dose,' said Gomer, 'but he said it was a tricky mixture. Misery, said Caney, who is a fair hand with an axiom when he tries, has been our favourite tipple for so long it will take a thousand years of experiment with applied gladness to dispel the flavour.'

Uncle Edwin was pointing again. His eye had the aptitude of hawks for singling out significant figures in crowds. 'Isn't that Caney the Cure over there now, Gomer? He's waving at you.'

A man with the hair style of Lloyd George at his bushiest was making his way towards us, holding aloft a stick carved like a totem pole. He had prodded a few voters with this stick to get them out of the way and a few of these people were following Caney with angry faces and telling him to be careful. Caney was gasping and agitated.

'What is it, Mr Caney?' asked Gomer.

'The stuff I gave you for Coleman.'

'The balm,' said four or five voices.

A grimace flashed across the face of Caney the Cure of which we could all taste the unhappiness.

'Balm, balm,' he said, as if trying to reassemble the fragments of a dream that had that very instant been kicked to death. 'I'll tell you about that. The stuff I gave to Coleman wasn't the soul balm after all.'

A wreath of grave expressions formed around Caney and the deep, cautionary voices of the Meadow Prospect group rolled out like drums: 'Buck up, Caney.' 'Have a care there, Kitchener.' 'This is no talk for a magician.'

Caney chuckled but there was no hint of amusement or flippancy in it. We could see that Caney meant this chuckle to be symbolic, a hint that this kind of idiot laughter was the last kiss and farewell of the tragic impulse, that all things, death, love, the senseless plume of space and stars, would all at last come to rest in some kind of cut-rate giggle.

'My wife made a mistake with the gummed label on the bottle. We have a lot of labels and my wife does a lot with the gum because my tongue tickles. She's a fine woman, my wife, but the taste of gum makes her giddy.'

We were all nodding in the most compassionate way because the mention of anyone in a fix even with stuff like gum brought us running up with our sympathy at the ready and fanning away for all we were worth. We urged Caney with our eyes to go on with his statement.

Caney chuckled again, but Uncle Edwin told him that he had our permission to remain sombre.

'That was some very funny stuff that Coleman took actually,' said Caney.

Uncle Edwin put his hand on Caney's shoulder as if to tell him that we were with him all the way, that if Cynlais should now drop down dead before he should even hear the starting gun of Erasmus John the Going Gone, the fact was simply that the angry rat that paces around and around at the heart of the life force had just given Caney one with its shorter teeth, that Coleman and that wrong mixture had been speeding towards each other through space since the moment when the absurd had decided to mould a whole species in its own image. Uncle Edwin tried with very quiet words to make these ideas plain to Caney. But either his words were too quiet or Caney had been too long in traffic with herbs to operate properly in a social context. He looked blank.

We all looked to Gomer Gough. We expected him, after a minute or two of preparation, to peel the ears of Caney with a jet of Old Testament wrath. But Gomer was just looking towards the part of the field where Cynlais and the other runners were reporting to Erasmus John and a clutch of other voters with badges and bits of paper. When he spoke it was in a voice of such softness we were glad that our cult of hymn-singing at all hours had left us with pity sleek and trained as a greyhound on the leash.

'Cynlais is out there, Mr Caney, faced with the hardest race of his life. His running knicks are ill-cut and will expose him to ridicule if not to prosecution. He is flanked by a biased and malevolent body of starters and judges who are not above giving orders to have Coleman strangled with the finishing tape if he should happen to come in first. On top of that, the libido of Coleman is tigerish and currently his head is between the tiger's teeth. His girl is that element with the red blouse standing at the foot of that flagpole. She is five square feet of licence and her name is Moira Hallam. A few minutes ago she gave him a laugh that for sheer contempt and coldness would have frozen a seal. Now you tell me, very jocose, that he has some sinister herb under his belt. What is it?'

'A stirring draught for lazy kidneys,' said Caney, very softly.

'Speak up, Caney,' called the voters on the outer fringe of the group, and Caney repeated what he had said, taking off his slouch in case this might be muffling some of the sound.

'How will it take him?' asked Gomer. 'This draught, how does it operate?'

'It varies,' said Caney. 'Sometimes when it begins its healing work there is a flash of discomfort, and I have known surprised clients come back to me hopping.'

'Hopping? What do you mean, hopping? Let's have the truth, Caney.'

'One leg seems to leave the ground as if trying to kick the kidneys into a brighter life.'

We all drew more closely around Caney and said very quietly: 'Duw, duw, duw!', which was a way we had of invoking God without committing ourselves unduly.

We turned to the part of the field where the sprint was shortly to begin. Erasmus John was entering into the brutal phase of his life as an official. He was dissatisfied with the rate at which the athletes had been coming out of the pavilion and he was prodding the various runners into position with his gun. He was putting some of them, including Cynlais Coleman, on edge and they were threatening to go home if Erasmus did not point the barrel of his weapon the other way.

'The only boy he isn't prodding with that flintlock,' said Milton Nicholas, 'is his own favourite, Keydrich Cooney, that red-thatched, chunky element on the side there, with a scalloped vest and the general bearing of a tamed ape. His speciality used to be cross-country events on muddy terrain and a chance to shove slower rivals into lonely ditches. But he emerged as a runner in sprints when he outpaced two bailiffs who were trying to shove an affiliation writ into Cooney's pocket. Erasmus John will handicap Cooney forward until he is practically biting the tape when the gun goes. See how he's edging on now while Erasmus keeps the other runners in a sweat of anxiety. What Herod did for child welfare Erasmus John will do for foot-racing.'

The gun went off. The crowd surged forward around me and I could see nothing of the race's details. Then there was a shout and a groan and I saw Cynlais Coleman shoot into the air, well in sight even above the taller heads around me. I jumped, too, to see if there was any sign of fresh smoke from Erasmus John's gun because Cynlais looked to me as if he had been shot. For a second the crowd broke and in the gap I saw the red head of Cooney flash past the tape.

It was not until that evening that I learned with any accuracy what had happened. We had led Cynlais home between us. He had refused to get out of his running costume and he looked shattered. He refused to say a word. After we had delivered him to his home we met at Tasso's Coffee Tavern.

Normally when we went into Tasso's the conversation was in full cry even before Tasso got his hand on the hot-water tap. But that night every topic seemed to be lying dead just behind us. Gomer Gough and Uncle Edwin stared at each other, at Tasso and then at themselves in the gleaming side of the urn. Tasso was very much slower than usual getting to work on the taps. He took down a large bottle, fished into it and brought out a wrapped toffee.

'Accept this rum-and-butter toffee, Mr Gough,' said Tasso. 'It will sweeten your mood.' He waited until Gomer had the sweet in his mouth and the first traces of softening in his eye as the sugar struck his palate. 'And what was the foot-race like, Mr Gough? What befell Mr Coleman the Comet?'

For a few moments Gomer could not marshal his words. Then, as the voters of Meadow Prospect often do when they have some outrage to describe, he highlighted some of the principal incidents of his story, with gestures as broad and dramatic as the size of Tasso's shop and the position of the urn would allow.

First he dropped into a crouching position on the floor to invoke the image of Cynlais making ready for the start.

Tasso leaned over the counter, concerned, and Uncle Edwin had to tell him that Gomer was all right, just acting. Then Gomer jumped erect, with a cruel, arrogant look on his face to imitate Erasmus John. Gomer's arm was outstretched and his index finger was working violently on an imaginary trigger. He had his hand pointed at the door. Three customers outside peered through the door's glass panel, saw Gomer, and moved up the street, at speed, thinking that Tasso had now had what for a long time had been coming to him, encouraging such clients as Gomer Gough and Uncle Edwin. Tasso told Uncle Edwin that he thought Gomer had now made his point and would he please point whatever it was he was supposed to have in his hand at some other part of the shop.

'In their long history, Tasso, the Celts have done some dubious and disastrous bits of running, but this thing today opened up a new path altogether. Erasmus John the Going Gone, that auctioneer who acts as an official at these events, fired his gun. Cynlais flashed into action and for five seconds he went so fast everybody thought he had left by way of Erasmus' gun. Didn't he, Edwin?'

'Fact,' said Edwin. 'He seemed to be in flight from all the world's heartbreak and shame.'

'Then Caney's cure struck,' said Gomer, and you could almost see the rum-and-butter toffee parting in his mouth to make way for the bitterness of his tone. 'Have you, Tasso, ever seen a man trying to finish a hundred-and-twenty-yard dash on one leg?'

'Not on one leg. Always in Italy both the legs are used.'

'It was a terrible sight. Cynlais gave some fine hops, I'll say that for him. On that form I'd enter him against a team of storks, but against those other boys he was yards behind. And that Erasmus John the Going Gone running alongside and asking sarcastically if Cynlais would like the stewards to do something about the leg he still had on the ground. I fancied I also saw Erasmus taking a few sly kicks at Cynlais as if he wished to further desolate the parts of the boy's spirit that hadn't yet been laid flat by Caney.'

'And where is he now, the Cynlais?' asked Tasso.

'In bed, trying to explain to his kidneys, which are still moving about inside him like jackie jumpers, about Caney, Caney's wife and her reaction to the gum on the labels that plays such hell with her.'

'It was Moira Hallam that did it,' said Uncle Edwin, sounding as angry as a minor key human being ever will. 'Compared with this business of physical love the Goodwin sands are a meadow. I'd like to make her sorry for the way she flicks acid over the hearts of boys like Cynlais.'

Gomer seconded this, and Tasso did something to set the urn hissing, which was his way of saying that he was behind the motion too.

The following night Milton Nicholas came into the Library and Institute and after a short spell of walking about among the bookshelves and thinking hard about the carnivals, went into the small anteroom where Gomer Gough and Teilo Dew the Doom were locked in a game of chess that seemed to have been going on for several winters.

'I've been thinking about Ephraim Humphries the iron-monger,' said Milton. Gomer Gough and Teilo Dew did not look up or seem surprised. Humphries had for years lived out on a kind of social tundra and his fiats against the pagans of Meadow Prospect were always high on the agenda of the Discussion Group. Ephraim was very comfortably off and he had a great weakness for budgerigars of which he had a front room full. He had three of these birds that could do rough versions of temperance hymns and missionary anthems like 'Row for the shore, sailor, pull for the shore, Heed not that stranded wreck but bend to the oar.' And he had one bird, a very strong, loud performer which had learned the first two bars of the 'Hallelujah Chorus', but this had done something to the bird's tail feathers and it had died. Ephraim's cordial urges had been cooled long since by handling so much cold metal in a shop full of draughts, and he really didn't see why the average human should want to eat, wander or love more than the average budgerigar.

'You know that Ephraim is moral adviser to the carnival committee,' said Milton.

'Yes, we know,' said Gomer. 'Those two bruises on his brow he got from two faints he had when watching Georgie Young's women's band, the Britannias.'

'That's it. He ranks nudity above war as a nuisance. I was at a short meeting tonight after tea. The regional carnival committee. Ephraim was there with a cutting edge. Most of what he said was about his visit last week to the Tregysgod carnival. If he ever gets the sight of

Cynlais Coleman and his boys out of his mind his mind will go with it. As for the Britannias he says it's time Georgie Young changed their costume to that of women in purdah so that they can operate from behind some kind of thick screen. But his main phobia is about Coleman, because Willie Silcox the Psyche kept interrupting that Ephraim's obsession with the way the wind kept blowing the Union Jacks against the bodies of the Britannias and showing up their shapes meant that Ephraim was working up to the sexual climax of the century, and that as soon as he caught the Britannias without their gazookas he would proceed to some act of massive ravishment and he would spend the rest of his life dancing on Calvin's grave. At this point that lecherous and bell-like baritone, Dewi Dando the Ding and the Dong, said that if Ephraim did any dancing on Calvin's grave after a session of roistering with those girls in the Britannias it would be strictly by proxy through four bearers. This enraged Ephraim and you could see from his face that his mind had been wallowing a bit in the notions sketched forth by Silcox so he changed tack and stuck to Cynlais Coleman. He's convinced now that what Fawkes was to parliament Coleman is now to morals, a one and fourpenny banger waiting for November. That gave me an idea of how we might get Ephraim to help us.'

'Put a light to Coleman's fuse and shock Humphries out of his wits, you mean?'

'No, no, no! Nothing like that at all.'

'But isn't Humphries dead against the bands? Isn't his task to morally advise them clean out of existence?'

'Not altogether. He says that while they strike him as pretty squalid, if they take people's minds off class rancour, agnosticism and the Sankey award, he's for them, always hoping for the day, he says, when the people generally will find the same release he does in a good funeral or a long argument about Baptism. So why don't we approach Humphries and explain that Cynlais and his boys are puritans at heart and want nothing better than to get hold of some decent, God-fearing costumes so that they can turn out looking less repulsive and frightening to the pious. We could also add that Cynlais has given up his old promiscuity since he came across Moira Hallam and swallowed that draught of Caney's cure. Then we can tap Humphries for some cash. He must have a soft side to his nature or he wouldn't keep all those birds in his front room.'

Teilo Dew and Gomer stared at the chessboard and the stagnant pieces as if they found this game as inscrutable as they had always found Humphries.

'Your mind's just singing, Milton,' said Gomer. 'From what I know of Humphries he probably keeps those birds in his front room just to test for gas. When the birds die Humphries changes the potted shrubs and chalks up a new cautionary text on the wall. He was the grumpiest boy I ever met behind a counter, although I will say that iron at all levels is a pretty sombre trade. He was the one ironmonger who sold paraffin that put out the match. But let's go and see him anyway.'

Gomer and Milton left Teilo to brood over the blockage

in the chess game and picked up Uncle Edwin who was sitting in the Reading Room humming a mossy old funeral chant over a brassily authoritative leading article in a national paper that was open in front of him. He invited Gomer and Milton to scan this article. They rushed their eyes down it. The writer had been dealing with the carnival bands and frankly felt that there was something potentially threatening to the State in having such masses of men, with nothing better to do, moving about the streets in march time. He suggested that a monster carnival to end all carnivals be organised, set it in motion with a strong platoon of Guards in the rear to ensure no getaways, then keep the whole procession in motion until it reached the South Pole where they could swap bits of political wisdom with the penguins. When Gomer and Milton finished reading the article they joined Uncle Edwin in humming the last verse of the funeral chant, coming out clearly with the words of the last line which praised the dignity and cheapness of the grave.

'But never mind about that now,' said Gomer. 'Milton has an idea that Ephraim Humphries might supply the money to drag Coleman and his band up into the temperate zone.'

Edwin was not enthusiastic. He said about the only thing he could recommend in the case of Humphries was a load of hot clinker for the man's bleaker and colder urges, but he responded to the glow of enthusiasm in Milton Nicholas' face and we started the journey across the town to the house of Ephraim Humphries.

Humphries lived in one of a group of larger houses on some high ground just outside the town's west side. There was a diamond-shaped pane of dark blue glass in the centre of his door which created an effect exactly halfway between sadness and intimidation. After our first knock we could see Humphries and his wife take up position in the passageway. They peered out at us and it was plain they felt no happiness or confidence at the sight of us. There was an open fanlight above the door through which we could hear most of what they said. They were speaking in whispers but whispers bred on long years in oratorio.

'I count four,' we heard Mrs Humphries say, 'but there may be more arranged on either side of the door.'

'Stop fearing the worst, Harriet,' said Humphries. 'You've never been the same since that lecturer told you your great-grandfather had had his bakehouse cooled in the Chartist troubles. Who are these fellows?'

'Can't tell for sure. There's a shady look about them.'

'That's the blue glass. My own father, seen through that diamond, looks as if he's just come running from the County Keep.'

'I told you you should never have accepted that invitation to go to those carnivals as adviser on morals. These are probably some louts you've offended with your straight talk about how bruises have now taken the place of woad as a darkening element on the moral fabric of the Celt. These men are very likely a group sent here by Cynlais Coleman, the leading dervish, to do you some mischief.' Her tone became strained and sharply informative. 'Do you know that the very word assassin comes from the Middle East where Coleman has his spiritual home. Let's bar the doors.' She made a quick move towards the door and there was a shifting of iron such as we would never normally hear outside a gaol.

'Stop being such a teacher, Harriet,' said Humphries. 'And throw those bolts back. I'd never have had them if they hadn't come to me cheap through the trade.'

The door was opened.

'What is it?' asked Humphries, showing only his head.

'We'd like a word with you, Mr Humphries,' said Gomer, and he gave us the cue with his hand to start smiling in the broadest, most unmalicious way we could manage. This performance was so out of tune with the mood of the times that Mrs Humphries, thinking from the lunatic look of us that we were out to kill them on more general grounds than she had imagined, tried to drag Humphries back into the passage and ram the bolts back home. He threw her off.

'Come on into the front room,' he said, his voice rustling with caution.

We moved slowly behind Humphries into the most tightly packed front parlour we had ever seen. On the wall, frame to frame, as if a broad gap would only aggravate the loneliness that had tormented and killed them on earth, were huge photographs of the most austere voters, a lot of them bearded and all of them frowning and staring straight at Humphries and us.

'Beloved pastors on the right-hand wall and irreplaceable

relatives on the left,' said Humphries as he saw us trying to map the great patches of gloom created by those faces. It struck us that with all these elements speaking up for the Black Meadow and the County Assizes on his flank he must have been driven into the ironmongery trade by centuries of inherited ill-feeling about the species. The furniture of the room, and it seemed from the amount of it that Humphries and his wife had both thrown a front-room suite into the marriage chest, was thick with plush and chenille. It made the whole chamber look like the hidden badge of all the world's outlawed or discouraged sensuousness. Our fascinated fingers kept reaching out and stroking the stuff until Humphries, looking convinced that we were all going to unpick and make off with a length of chenille to eke out the costumes of a carnival band, told us to stop it and get to the point. Around the room were eight or nine birdcages and we watched the birds inside with great interest. There might have been a time when the budgerigars had thought of trying to give some light relief to those divines and relatives in the photographs but they had broken their beaks on all that ambient gravity and lost. They now sat on their perches looking as sad and damned and muffled as the gallery of perished censors. Their singing had been soaked futilely into the layers of plush and they had shut up. As we squeezed into the tiny areas of free floor space, with Mrs Humphries pushing hard at Uncle Edwin because she did not fancy the idea of any of our delegation being left with her in the passageway, one of the birds let out a note. It was not gay or musical. It was like the first note of the last post in a low-grade military funeral, heard through rain and trees. It sounded as if the bird thought we had come to bail him out.

Humphries looked up at the bird and said:

'You hear that? You hear that? They might come yet.'

'Oh, nice birds,' said Milton Nicholas with real rapture in his voice. We admired Milton for this because we had never before heard a word of interest, let alone praise, from him on the subject of birds. Once in the Discussion Group he had gone so far as to praise the habit of migration and wheeling off south at the approach of autumn as a tactically sound approach and one which, he hoped, would be copied when man resolved the last cramp of tribal idiocy and took the whole world as his available playground. Milton won his motion that night on the rheumatic vote alone, because there was a whole fleet of voters present stiffened up by winter rains and as badly in need of a stronger sun as of a more encouraging govern-ment. Later, Milton qualified those words of approval about birds by saying that he considered pigeon fancying, which at the time was running neck and neck with sex as a life form among the more torpid prolies, a very lulling activity and worthy to be classed as opium for those people who had somehow managed to emerge awake from under the long, soporific cone of our traditional prescriptions.

Humphries let his eyes go right around the room, nodding at each of the cages.

'Would that men were more like them. So bright, so brief, so harmless, and no sorrow in their singing.'

'You're right, boy,' said Milton. 'Good and deep as the singing has been in most of our chapels, I think we've overdone the note of death and desperation in certain types of cadence.' He pointed at the cage of the bird that had let out the solitary note. 'Give us the same seed and the same sure accommodation and we'd be there with the budgies.'

Milton's reference to the chapel singing and the slightly demagogic tilt of the last sentence had made Humphries very wary again.

'Your business, gentlemen?'

'We want to thank you,' said Gomer, 'for the fine stand you made at Tregysgod and the remarks you made about Cynlais Coleman's band. We think the same. Those home-grown dervishes have cancelled out the landing of Augustus. We are collecting among ourselves to fit Coleman and his men out in such a way that they will not cause the very hillsides to blush as they do now. Could you help us?'

Humphries stood stock still for at least two minutes, his lips drawn in and his eyes fixed hypnotically on the most forbidding of the portraits. Uncle Edwin muttered to Gomer that someone should give Humphries an investigatory push in case he had chosen this moment to die just to put us in the wrong. But Humphries came suddenly back to life, shaking his head as if recovering from some spell laid upon him by the granite features of the voter in the portrait.

'That was my uncle, Cadman Humphries,' he said, his

voice still a little muffled, uncertain. We remembered Cadman. He had been a quarry-owner, the only quarry owner whose face had made his employees think they were working double time or made them constantly doubtful about where they should place the explosive charge.

'As a matter of fact I could and will help you,' he said. His voice was now loudly vibrant and overwhelming. Four of the birds came rushing to the bars of their cage and Uncle Edwin pressed his body against the plush flank of a settee to mute the effect of Humphries' outburst. 'It will be my great pleasure to do so. I am vice president of a committee which is gathering funds to supply wholesome entertainments for the valley folk during this emergency. Just in case these carnivals should become a permanent part of our lives we must at least see that minimum standards of decorum are accepted, and that the marchers are decently covered against both wind and temptation. As for Coleman, whose first appearance before my wife gave her such hiccups as would take a lagoon of small sips to cure, I will leave it to you men to think out an alternative costume for this buffoon and you may leave the bill, within reason, to me. Nothing too royal or lavish, of course.'

'Of course,' said Gomer. 'By the way, Mr Humphries, have you seen Georgie Young's women's band, the Britannias?'

Humphries' eyes became a twitch of embarrassed guilt and he whipped back around to face Cadman Humphries and to salute the need for a really stony ethic in a softening world.

'I'm afraid I haven't had a good look at them. I've heard about them and I've had some good reports of Mr Georgie Young's excellent work as a driller. But I haven't really seen them. Last week at Tregysgod, for some reason they didn't arrive as far as the judges' stand.'

'Take a good look at them, Mr Humphries. When you see them you'll lose what is left of your hair. Then you'll start another fund to have Young hung and the bands-women treated with balsam of missionary.'

Milton tugged at Gomer, thinking that any more talk that Humphries might construe as being morally double-jointed and we would be getting the boot. But Mr Humphries did not seem put out. Through his eyes I thought I could now see a film of comfortable steam above his thoughts. We said thank you and goodnight.

'Goodnight,' said Humphries. 'I'm surprised to find you men so helpful, such watchdogs in the cause of whole-someness.'

'Just let us catch a whiff of anything that isn't whole-some, Mr Humphries,' said Milton Nicholas, 'then watch us bark and bite.'

We went straight from the house of Ephraim Humphries to that of Cynlais Coleman. Cynlais' mother, a ravelled woman whose fabric, even without Cynlais, would not have stood up to too much wear and tear, took us instantly to Cynlais' bedroom, glad to be sharing her problem. Cynlais was in bed, flattened under the load of his grief and a big family Bible, trying to reassemble the fragments of himself after the two disasters. We were puzzled by the Bible and were going to ask Mrs Coleman whether she had meant it just to keep Cynlais in bed and off his feet, but she explained that she had given it to him to read the Book of Job to help him keep his troubles in proportion, but Cynlais had kept flicking the pages and referring to Moira Hallam as Delilah, and saying that Job seemed to have come right out of one of the blacker Thursday night sessions at the Discussion Group in the Institute.

At the sight of us Cynlais drew the Bible and the bed-clothes up to his face as if to hide.

'Hullo Cynlais,' said Gomer. 'Big news, boy. We've got the money for the new costumes. What fancies have you got on this subject, and for goodness' sake keep inside Europe this time because we're hoping to have enough to cover you all from top to bottom.'

There was now nothing of Cynlais except his very small brow, and he had his hands clenched over the sides of the Bible as if he were thinking of throwing it at Gomer as a first step to clearing the bedroom. Uncle Edwin, at the foot of the bed, knocked solemnly on Cynlais' tall foot as if it were a door.

'Come on, Cynlais,' he said. 'Buck up, boy, and stop looking so shattered. This isn't the end of the world; it's only the first crack.'

Cynlais' whole face came into view. It was grey, shrunken and lined. Uncle Edwin said that between Caney's kidney-whipper and carnal wishes it was clear that Coleman had been through the mill.

'I keep thinking of what Moira told me,' said Cynlais,

with a look in his eye that made Milton Nicholas say that Caney should be held on charges of making a public mischief.

'What did she say?' asked Gomer.

'She said, "Cynlais, has your heart ever been in the orange groves of Seville?"'

We all tried to relate this statement to the carnivals and the news we had brought from Ephraim Humphries.

'You can't possibly have a band of marching oranges,' said Gomer. 'Just drop this greengrocery motif, Cynlais. You can be too subtle in these matters. Look what happened to those Eskimos from the top of the valley. You remember their manoeuvre of shuddering at the end of every blast from the gazookas to show extreme cold and the need for blubber, no one ever understood it. They shuddered themselves right out of the carnival league.'

'I don't mean oranges,' said Cynlais. 'I mean bullfighters, with me dressed up in the front as an even better bullfighter than Moelwyn Cox.'

We had to move away from the bed at this point and explain in low voices to Milton Nicholas about Moelwyn Cox and his appearance with the Birchtown Amateur Operatic company as the matador Escamillo. Milton's first impulse on hearing Cynlais make this reference to bullfighters was to think that Cynlais, between the weight of that Bible and the bushfires of his lustful wanting, had been flattened and charred into madness. Cynlais, with a glare of one hundred per cent paranoia, told us to stop whispering or get out of his bedroom.

Gomer went back to the bedside and shook Cynlais gravely by the hand.

'That's a wonderful idea, Cyn,' he said. 'Come over to Tasso's tomorrow night and we'll talk it over. Do you think you can manage it?'

Cynlais said at first that without some word of encouragement and hope from Moira Hallam he would never again leave that bedroom except to show the rent collector that he was not a subtenant. But we got him out of the bed and marched him around the room a few times, taking it in turns to catch him when his legs buckled. We all agreed that he would be able to do the trip to Tasso's on the following evening with a few attendant helpers on his flank.

Willie Silcox was in Tasso's the next day. He was interested when we told him about our visit to Ephraim Humphries, and he made notes when he heard about the various quirks of body, face and thought we had noted in Humphries when we mentioned the Britannias.

'One of these nights,' said Willie, 'Humphries will draw a thick serge veil over the portrait of Cadman Humphries, the quarry owner whose eyes and brows keep Ephraim in a suit of glacial combinations, and he will slip forth into the darkened street, just like Jack the Ripper, but knifeless and bent on a blander type of mischief altogether than was Jack. And you say he's going to foot the bill for a new band for Coleman? That will bring him closer to the physical reality of these carnivals and allow his senses a freer play. What is this new band going to be called?'

'The Meadow Prospect Toreadors, Willie. What do you think of that?'

'Very nice, very exotic. It will help to show what little is left of our traditional earnestness to the gate but good luck to you all the same. We are headed for an age of clownish callousness and we might as well have a local boy as stage hand in that process as anyone else. These bullfighters will bring the voters an illusion of the sun and a strong smell of marmalade, both much needed.'

Gomer turned to Mathew Sewell the Sotto who was putting Tasso's teeth on edge by beating his tuning fork on the counter and bringing its pointed end sharply into play on the metal edge of the counter.

'What about the theme tune for these boys when Cynlais gets his new band started, Mathew? What do you suggest?'

Sewell thought for a whole minute in silence, then brought his tuning fork across his teeth as if to bring his reflections to the boil.

'Something Spanish, of course,' said Sewell, and Gomer told him to try his tuning fork on his teeth again to see if he could come out with something more cogent.

'Try to make it something operatic, Mr Sewell,' said Cynlais Coleman, who had come in five minutes before wearing a long raincoat and the visor of his cap hiding the most significant parts of his face. It had taken some major wheedling to get him to shed this disguise. He sat now by the stove looking overt and edgy.

'What did you say?' asked Gomer.

'Something operatic,' said Cynlais. 'I want to show that

Moira Hallam that I'm as cultured as Moelwyn Cox. What about that Toreador Song? That's a treat. That was what Moelwyn made such a hit with. Let's have that.'

Mathew Sewell ignored Cynlais except for a short glance that told him to pick up his cap and get back out of sight.

'It will have to be something Spanish of course. There are strong affinities between Iberian music and our own and I don't see why we shouldn't exploit this. I can make it marks for you if ever I'm one of the judges. Did you know, Tasso, that we were once known as Iberian Celts?'

Tasso said no very politely, but we could see from his mouth that he was tired of having Sewell pitching on him with questions that were so well outside the catering trade.

There was a long silence from Sewell and Tasso worked the urn to cover his embarrassment.

'What about the Toreador Song?' asked Cynlais again.

'Just sing it over,' said Sewell very casually, as if to say that we might as well have something going on while he picked down the one he wanted from a hallful of Iberian alternatives.

Cynlais started in a tenor so thin he had us all bending over him to follow the melody. Cynlais had never been a vigorous singer, and his collapse had caused his cords to dangle worse than ever. We all gathered around him and tried as briskly as we could to give him support in the bull-fighter's song.

Tasso tapped with his toffee hammer on the counter and smiled broadly at Sewell as if to tell him that this was just the thing, especially if played or sung without Gomer

Gough, who was lunging at the melody as recklessly as he would have done at the bull.

'No,' said Sewell. 'I don't think so. It's a little bit too complicated to play on the march. We want something a bit witless, something everybody'll know.'

'What about "I'm One of the Nuts of Barcelona"?' asked Gomer Gough, and the title of this piece sounded strangely from the mouth of Gomer, which had been worn down to the gums by the reading of a thousand unsmiling agendas.

'What's nutting to do with bullfighting?' asked Uncle Edwin. 'Let's lift the tone of these carnivals. I'm for the operatic tune. Let's go through it again. It's got a very warming beat, although I still think a nation that has to make the fighting of bulls a national cult is just passing the time on and trying to keep its mind off something else.' Uncle Edwin gave Cynlais a nod and raised his hand to lead the group back into Bizet.

'Don't make difficulties, Edwin,' said Gomer, and he was clearly torn between two conversational lines; one to censure Edwin for hanging a little close to the boneyard spiritually; second, to explain to us how he had come to spare enough time from the dialectic to find the title of such a tune as 'I'm One of Nuts of Barcelona', one of the least pensive lyrics of the period. But Willie Silcox nipped in before Gomer could make his point.

'There's another thing, too,' said Willie. 'Do you still want Cynlais to win the esteem of Moira Hallam?'

'Oh definitely. It'll give Cynlais that little extra bit of winning vim. What are you hinting at now, Silcox?'

'This girl has got some sort of Spanish complex.'

'No question about it,' said Mathew Sewell. He turned to Tasso. 'I expect you've heard, Tasso, that the adjective Spanish is often used in connection with various sexual restoratives and stimulants.' But he got no answer. Tasso was not looking. 'She's even got me feeling like a bit of a picador, and I haven't felt that sort of urge very often since I conducted the united choirs of Meadow Prospect in the Messiah three years ago.' Sewell paused and his thoughts dived into waters that were not instantly visible to us. 'Do you remember those sopranos in their snow-white blouses? Do you remember the big dispute about my treatment of the last six hallelujahs?'

We remembered the sopranos, the steep, tumescent tiers of gleaming satin, the last great outlay on sheet music and cloth in the pre-bath-chair phase of the coal trade in the third decade. But we could recall no dispute about Sewell's interpretation of that particular score. His hallelujahs had seemed to us orthodox, even flatly so.

Gomer became annoyed at this backwash of recollection in which we had politely allowed ourselves to become involved. He accused Sewell of egomania, of putting his own and Handel's past before Meadow Prospect's future, of creating confusion and making our thinking bitty. Cynlais Coleman, at best a staccato thinker, and always prone to be hypnotised by Sewell, queried this.

'Anyway,' said Gomer, 'carry on, Willie, with your remarks about Moira Hallam.'

'What better than to have her walking right in front

of Coleman's new band, dressed up as Carmen?' asked Willie.

He addressed his question to Sewell, but there was no reply from him. He was in the cold mental vaults of his memories of the Messiah, that white acreage of banked sopranos, and his treatment of those shouts of praise.

'That's a first-class notion, Willie,' said Gomer. 'Paolo,' he said to Tasso, 'give Willie Silcox another raspberry cordial. He's the Livingstone of our mental Congo.'

During the next week the bullfighting uniforms for Cynlais and his band were stitched from cheap cloth and rough recollections of Blood and Sand, a film which had been screened at one of our cinemas, The Cosy, a year before. On a reasonably flat part of the waun the band practised its marching and playing. The wind came down to us scalloped by the sharp, quick step beat of 'The Nuts of Barcelona'.

We were full of hope for Cynlais and his boys. We needed that hope. A week before the great Trecelyn carnival at which Cynlais was to make his first appearance with his matadors, the Sons of Dixie had registered their tenth total defeat in a row at a town called Elmhill. They had gone to Elmhill with an arrogant faith in themselves and sure of triumph. Georgie Young the Further Flung had drilled them more ruthlessly than ever, and at their last rehearsal he had wept with pride at the sight of their speed and precision. Under heavy pressure he had decided to abandon his phobic faith in an all-black turn out and the wives of the Dixie's had laundered their trousers and shirts into an incredible snowiness and that gentle, theatrically minded voter Festus Phelps the Fancy, who was in general control of décor in our stretch of the valley, had blackened their faces with an especially yielding type of cork down to the very soul of sable.

So confident had we become in the Sons of Dixie before they set out for Elmhill that all the people in Windy Way, the long, hillside street that pushed its grey, apologetic track right up to the summit of Merlin's Brow, got candles and lighted them as soon as darkness fell on the day of the carnival. The candles were placed on the front windowsill of most of the two hundred houses in Windy Way and as the street, seen from the bottom of Meadow Prospect, seemed to go right off into the sky the small flames made a beautiful and moving sight, and we all thought that this would be a fine way of greeting the Sons of Dixie when they drummed and gazookered their return in glory to Meadow Prospect. But they lost all the same. 'Unimaginative.' 'Prussian and aesthetically Luddite.' 'Naïve and depressing.' These were just some of the judges' verdicts, and Georgie Young was carried back on some sort of litter a full hour before the band itself returned.

The Sons of Dixie came back in the darkness. Some sympathisers had staked them to a gill or two. They marched through the town and halted at the foot of Windy Way when their leader, Big Mog Malley, so erect even in the florescent melancholy of the moment he looked as if he had done a spell of training with Frederick the Great before moving under the baton of Georgie Young, raised his gigantic staff and told them to break ranks. Their mood as they stared up at the long legion of triumphant candles was for some bit of self-defensive clowning. They found they were quite near the work-yard of our undertaker, Goronwy Mayer the Layer. The lads pushed open Mayer's gate. The locks and bolt were brittle because Mayer believed that everything connected with death should be friendly and easily negotiable. They commandeered a hearse. An unbelievable number of them managed to clamber aboard and they began their journey with that erratic reciter, Theo Morgan the Monologue, at the wheel and keeping his head bent in comical sorrow until the hearse hit the kerb and jerked a couple of the Dixies on to the roadway. Some gazooka players fell in behind and struck up with a funeral hymn so magical in its scope for sensuous harmony it had caused many a mourner to forget the body. Mayer the Layer came out of his house full of fury at the sight of his burglared yard but he had to follow behind saying not a word because he had taken a vow never to interfere in any way with the singing of that particular hymn because it had sent up the figures for funeral attendance a hundred per cent. Mayer even joined in loudly in the lower register. He had always said that had it not been for the excluding nature of his trade he could have done something as a baritone.

And with every yard advanced by that strange cortège a candle on its windowsill was extinguished by a housewife eager not to waste the tallow on an empty midnight and wishful not to seem to mock the Sons of Dixie in their hour of hollowness.

That memory made us all the more anxious as we watched Cynlais and his followers practise up on the flat moorland. It seemed that Cynlais' hour had come. The toreador role lifted him on to a plane of joyful release, and once the slower bandsmen had been persuaded that with this move into Spain 'Colonel Bogey' would be definitely out of place the musical side of it went well. Festus Phelps the Fancy created a bit of confusion during the early stages of preparation. Festus' attitude to the bands had been becoming steadily more antic as his power and influence as artistic adviser had increased. He had been delighted when Cynlais and his band had decided to become bullfighters because he had read many books about the bulls and rather fancied that he himself had the shape and style to have done well at this exercise. He felt this all the more keenly because a few years before Silcox and a group of fanciers at the Institute had told Phelps that he had the shape and look of Carpentier. He had one fight. He went into the ring, superbly handsome but totally inept in the use of his hands and attended by two of the least aware voters in Meadow Prospect who were to be his seconds. They believed that Festus would win by grace of footwork and they were still massaging Festus' feet when the first bell went. The opponent's opening view of Festus was a figure falling on his face for no reason that he could see. He helped Festus to his feet and set to work. Festus was in the ring twenty seconds, but that was only because the referee was a slow counter even when not doing it over the form of a man as prone and still as Festus was at that moment. Since then Festus had felt that in a sport like bullfighting he would find the right field for the passion and solitariness he knew to be his, without having the clumsy folly of his fellow men clogging the pipes of his talent every whip-stitch. So he tackled his advisory job with the Meadow Prospect Matadors like a crusader.

At a full meeting of the bandsmen at the Institute he explained to them the main movements of the bullfight, comparing them with the phases of a symphony to which he applied the proper Italian terms. Then he told them about the moment of truth, the moment at which the bullfighter faces the bull with a tension of courage that makes life imperishably resonant, when he slaps death's both cheeks and dares it to try on him any of the infamous betrayals whereby it had made shoddy and shuffling fools of the whole race of men. Festus, on the platform, looked right into death's eyes, taking a little time off now and then to throw looks of freezing contempt at the bandsmen whom he saw as the sweating, treacherous, contumelious ticket holders in the sun and the shadow. He rose on tiptoe to deliver the stroke of death to the grave-ripe beast which only he could see. The bandsmen, few of whom had heard Festus' talk from the beginning, were confused as never before and they thought that Festus' mind, without question one of the most sensitive in the division, had now been submitted to one aggravation too many and had broken loose from its last hinge. Some pointed end of revelation had jabbed Festus on to a high apocalyptic peak. All around him on the stage walked every privation and mishap that had ever driven him into his tight and terrifying corner of self-awareness, one last rubbed nerve between himself and the relief of a frank lunacy. 'What can be the flavour on the tongue of death, daft death?' he had shouted. 'What was that again?' asked a few of the bandsmen in the front row, and they started to fidget a bit as they got a glimpse of death as an articulate but loutish imbecile met casually in a lightless lane. Three committee men of the Institute, who were sitting in the back row, reminded Festus that questions of the raking, rattling sort he had just put to the matadors had to be reserved for the smaller, quieter rooms.

Then Festus, overcome by the beauty and mental nakedness of the moment, had broken down and was led weeping off the platform. Gomer Gough and Uncle Edwin were sent for from the Reading Room and were told of what had been going on. They got hold of four bandsmen, lined them up on the stage and told them to run through 'I'm One of the Nuts of Barcelona' twice. It took that and a short statement from Gomer Gough on the dangers of emotionalism to get the matadors back into mental motion.

Festus even then had not quite shot his bolt. Up on the practice ground he made a last effort to give an authentic Sevillian edge to what he thought the rather clomping approach of Cynlais' boys.

'The day of straightforward marching is done,' he said.

'In these carnivals we have the seed of a great popular ballet. You see into what ruin you run if you stick to the stolid conventions that have governed the carnivals so far. The Sons of Dixie marched with the dour determination of iron collared serfs and what did it get them. Half an acre of bunions and a threat of police court prosecution from Goronwy Mayer for dragging the paraphernalia of death into a context of gross buffoonery. No, what we want is a leap of imagination.'

He got his leap. It was built around the moment of truth.

At the end of the theme tune the band would stop dead and every gazooka would blow a long, loud, low note. That was supposed to be the final defiance of the bull. Then the matadors all stood on tiptoe and held their gazookas as if for the thrust of extinction. This manoeuvre was looked on with astonishment by all the supporters who watched the band rehearse up on the moorland. Either the matadors were a naturally flat-footed lot, or they held their gazookas too low, or they did not realise how tall a bull can be, but their posture was ambiguous and created a lot of unfavourable talk among those supporters who were anxious to keep the goodwill of the chapels.

Two days before the Trecelyn carnival we were walking down the hillside with Cynlais. About twenty yards behind us Festus Phelps was talking fast and passionately to half a dozen matadors who still did not know what he was supposed to be getting at. Of these voters there were four who had never been able to stand on tiptoe without a feeling of crucial absurdity, and they were telling Festus that after two efforts to rise like that and deal with the bull they would never again have the nervous calm to find the right note when the band struck up again with 'Barcelona'.

'That notion of stopping and lunging with the gazookas is going to play hell with the marching,' said Cynlais Coleman. 'I think that that Festus Phelps the Fancy has just been sent here to hinder us. Why didn't you tell him to leave us alone, Gomer?'

'Patience, Cyn. We can't afford to offend Festus yet. He's doing splendid work with the costumes. He's got the touch and the women who are doing the stitching say that he's got a peerless hand with the needle. But we mustn't allow him to overdo this mania for the ballet or we'll be badgering Ephraim Humphries for another grant, this time to have Festus removed. If he's going to develop fresh art forms for the people he should have a better team to play with than the matadors. There are some very bandy-legged boys among them and they seem to be even more so when they get up on their toes and get poised for the thrust. The bull would run right through.'

'What about Moira, Gomer? When is she going to start walking in front of the band like you said?'

'We're keeping her as a surprise. Don't worry, she'll be ready for the day. We've given her the beat of "I'm One of the Nuts" and she's been practising around the table in her front room. Sewell has been coaching her. The first time he walked in front of her round the front room table to give her an idea of the type of slink and wriggle he mentally associates with this element of Carmen. The second time Sewell went around the front room table behind her, and he felt his reserve ravelling and he had to sit down at Mrs Hallam's harmonium and play that version of "Abide with Me" that leaves no room for laughs. And don't forget, Cynlais. In the carnival you'll be walking behind her, too, and your gonads are still fresh-faced compared with Sewell's. So if your mother has any cooling herb in the house fill up on it before the big day.'

Cynlais stopped, opened his eyes wide and raised his arm. 'In that matador's uniform, Gomer, I'll be like a monk. Honest to God.'

The next night there was a big excited crowd in Tasso's Coffee Tavern. They had come there straight from the practice ground where Cynlais and the boys had rehearsed for the last time, in full Andalusian rig. It had been an exultant occasion and the committee men had marched alongside the band, keeping step and humming the theme tune. Gomer Gough was breathless as he leaned over Tasso's counter. He was in moderate funds after the sale of thirty bags of coal from his tiny unofficial outcrop mine near the top of Merlin's Brow. He gave Tasso a complicated order of fruit drinks for about half the bandsmen. Then he said to the whole shopful of matadors and supporters: 'Well, tomorrow's the day, the Trecelyn Competitive Inter-valley Festival.'

'What are the prospects, Mr Gough?' asked Tasso, leaning away from the urn, which was in top fettle.

'Never better,' said Gomer. 'You should see Cynlais.

Sideboards down to the chin, little moustache, a stiff, flattish black hat like Valentino but even flatter, I fancy, than that hat we saw Valentino wearing in that film down at The Cosy. And his every glance is a search for a bull. It took him a bit of time to remember that he was no longer the Mad Mahdi and to stop looking demented, but he's fine now.'

'And the Signorina Hallam?'

'You wouldn't believe! Carmen in the flesh. Red shawl, and we've collected so many combs to stick in her tall black hair there isn't a kempt head on our side of the Meadow. We've kept her dark so far because we don't want Ephraim Humphries to see her and start accusing her of goading the poor to ruin. Ephraim paid for most of the costumes and on questions of decorum he's touchier than a boil. Let's hope it's a very fine day tomorrow. Then Ephraim can put Moira down to a shimmer of heat.'

Tasso raised himself and spoke over the heads of the people who were standing in the shop.

'And how, Mr Sewell, are the ladies, the Britannias?'

We hadn't noticed Mathew Sewell sitting in the far corner and he advanced at our call from the corner and towards the counter with a cup of some dark, cold-looking liquid in his hand. He gave a deep groan. Just behind me Willie Silcox was whispering to Uncle Edwin that this groan we had just heard from Sewell was without question an echo of what Sewell had gone through in Moira Hallam's front room when he was getting her posture up to the mark.

'It's a fatal thing, Edwin, a fatal thing.'

'What is, Willie?' asked Uncle Edwin, who was exhausted by watching the final rehearsal and talking with Festus Phelps about the crass, anti-cultural attitude of Gough and Coleman. Uncle Edwin had not been listening at all attentively when Gomer had explained the day before about Sewell's visits to the home of Moira Hallam to give her secret instruction in being a Carmen. So Willie Silcox had Edwin foxed. 'What is, Willie?' he asked again, hoping that the blankness on his face would send Willie whispering to someone else.

'Playing "Abide with Me" on a small harmonium right on top of a mood of intense longing. I've known it bring down the whole mental scaffolding of voters before this.'

Uncle Edwin asked Tasso to turn up the steam of the urn to a point where it would blot out Silcox. Then we resumed our study of Sewell.

'Tasso,' said Sewell, 'slip another beef cube in this cup and warm the water up while I tell you about my troubles with those women, the Britannias. I've spent weeks trying to find out why they go so out of tune on "Rule, Britannia". If they were all brazen and defiant like their leader, that heavy, fierce woman, Maudie Gordon, I don't think they'd have any trouble. But there's a core of very shy women there, I'm sure, who must have been in a mood of strange brief frenzy when they signed up in the Britannias in the first place, and who still feel horrified when they find themselves out in the street with little more on than a single layer of thin Union Jack. They play out of tune to take the public's mind off how much they're showing. I've got five members of my madrigal group to march on each side of them, singing the melody loud and plain to keep them on the pitch, but I don't know how the judges will take to that tactic. I've chosen madrigal singers who don't open their mouths very wide and we'll have them edging in towards the Britannias from time to time as if they were members of the public, not to make the thing too obvious.'

Sewell took a quick, painful sip at his now quite hot drink, and while he blew loudly to cool his lips everybody in the shop chatted about the Britannias and what could be done to keep these women in tune. But Sewell waved them to silence as if that issue had now ceased to be important.

'But my biggest trouble now,' he said, 'is that drummer, Olga Rowe. I told Georgie Young from the start that he should have given Olga a much smaller drum. But he said it made a nice touch of pathos that made up to some extent for the many faults of the Britannias on the march. It's fine, he said, that big drum advancing on you with hardly anything of Olga in sight except her arms.'

'I've seen it,' said Uncle Edwin. 'It's uncanny. What's the matter with her?'

'She's been driven hysterical by the new pattern of vibrations set up in her by the drumming and now she gets a laughing fit every time she touches the pigskin. She keeps her husband out on the landing at nights because she's so sensitive and so easily set off. Her husband is that complaisant, uncomplaining little voter, Mogford Rowe. He says he doesn't mind sleeping upright and alone if it means getting away from Olga's tremors and being beaten black and blue to the rhythm of "Rule, Britannia". Even in sleep this Olga is on duty in the back row of the band.'

'A brisk tune, "Rule, Britannia",' said Gomer Gough, 'and damaging to marriage when heard without warning in bed.'

'Is Willie Silcox the Psyche here?' asked Sewell. 'Oh aye, there you are. Tell me, Silcox, what psychological approach would you recommend for a woman in such a fix as this Olga Rowe?'

'I don't know,' said Willie. 'I know this woman only from afar by the racket she makes banging on this instrument. And Freud, not often foxed, is silent about women being driven mad by their own drumming.'

'Never mind, though,' said Mathew. 'Of one thing at least we can all be certain. Whatever happens to Georgie Young and Olga Rowe, tomorrow will be Cynlais Coleman's day.'

But it was not to be. The prize was not to be ours. It was a day of oven heat and the wet hills under the unaccustomed shimmer seemed to be laughing with surprise. But the sun meant little to us for calamity trailed like a flag behind us all day long.

Georgie Young had been persuaded to let the Sons of Dixie have one last fling before hanging up their gazookas. Georgie had been hyper-tense for days and his daughter had alerted Peredur Parry the Pittance, the Public

Assistance official who was charged with the task of keeping an eye on the twin field of destitution and dementia among the voters. Georgie had been watching with a yellow eye the proud strut of Cynlais Coleman and the matadors and he was heard muttering to himself as he wandered around the bookshelves of the Institute looking for books about his idol, Kitchener:

'I'll give them bull. I'll give them toreador. I'll show that bloody Coleman. I owe it to Kitchener.'

So between resentment and a touch of late summer madness Georgie decided on a bold stroke. He told the Sons of Dixie to shed their white suits and fitted them with a tip-to-toe covering of cork stain and a kind of thick straw sash made from a thoroughly looted little rick on the land of Nathan Wilkins, the farmer. This was to give the effect of African warriors of the Lobengula epoch. The straw sashes were not easy to fasten and had the hard, abrasive quality of Wilkins himself. Besides, Wilkins had turned up with a shotgun to stand guard over the rick as they were helping themselves to material for the last twenty sashes, and there was a big feeling of insecurity among the boys wearing this last batch of coverings. The bandsmen were in trouble after the first dozen steps and overtly scratching in ways that the judges were bound to consider insanitary and ungracious. On top of that Georgie had decided that the Meadow Prospect Matabele, as he now called his followers, would march barefooted. He said it would be a tour de force to have them march with the same fury and dash as of old with nothing between their feet and the County Council highway, which could, in patches, be rough.

But the day of the carnival was against him. The sun had started to melt the macadam on the road by eleven in the morning and the marchers behind Big Mog Malloy were leaving a significantly deep spoor behind them. After the first mile the Matabele had a four-inch sole of asphalt, and those who were not actually keeling over were slowed down to a pathetic stumble and urging Mog Malloy to take his feather headdress off and use it and kill Young. To make things even cooler, council officials were up and down the flank of the warriors demanding their arrest for playing such hell with the road surface and making a rough assessment of the weight of macadam being carried by each bandsman. The Dixies were disqualified for holding up the carnival by sitting down on the roadside and using knives to chip off the macadam. They were disqualified under Rule 17 of the carnival code which stated that offensive weapons were not to be used on the march even to get back to bare feet. Sweat and anguish had streaked their cork stain into a dramatic leopard pattern.

The Britannia were early thrown into confusion by Olga Rowe tickling herself into the loudest laughing fit of this century. She had not been helped by having Sewell and the madrigal singers going up to her at short intervals arranged by Sewell and telling her: 'Olga, what you feel inside you, Olga, is joy, just joy.' And they would laugh in a way which for Olga was the cherry on the trifle. She was last seen drumming at forty miles an hour, down a side street, followed closely by a short old man with very fast legs. Some said this voter was the owner of the drum and off to get it back; others said he was a noted amorist out to take advantage of Olga Rowe's confusion.

The day had started well for the matadors. We had formed in a crowd outside Moira Hallam's house. Then Cynlais' band, a moving wall of red, yellow and black, giving out 'I'm One of the Nuts of Barcelona' with tremendous brio on their gazookas, had marched into the street. They blew a sort of fanfare which was Moira's cue. She came out of the front door like a sensational shout from a mouth. The crimson shawl set the whole street flaming and Moira's management of her body did as much for our senses. Moira had had her hair bunched up in a way that made her stubby body look rather top-heavy, but no one looked at her hair for long. Moira took up her position in front of the band.

Gomer Gough and the committee men led a little burst of clapping and this was the cue for that well-known gardener, Naboth Jenks the Pinks, to step forward with a rose of deep red and the biggest petals ever seen in Meadow. Jenks moved out of the crowd too abruptly and Moira stepped away from him thinking that Jenks was merely out to commit some act of sexual bravura. Then she saw the rose which Jenks had been holding behind his back and while she was marvelling at the size and perfume of it Gomer Gough, in his role of tireless chairman, was proposing a formal vote of thanks to Jenks for having evolved a rose with definite cauliflower overtones. Then

Gomer told Moira to put the rose in her mouth and keep it there. At first Moira did not like this idea and Mrs Hallam went right up to Gomer and told him about some uncle of hers who had been driven mad by nibbling at flowers. But Moira was persuaded that no one had ever seen an authentic Carmen without the rose in her mouth and very gingerly she placed the bloom between her big, strong teeth. The sight of her had a great effect and even Teilo Dew the Doom said later that even he, upon whose love life a heavy ice cap had fallen in the autumn of 1922, found himself gulping with desire as the red of the rose and the white of the teeth made their first impact.

Then there was a whistle from Cynlais and a flourish from his drum major's staff. The bandsmen raised their gazookas to the ready and on the down beat from Cynlais they began to play and moved off in the direction of Trecelyn. On the pavement the only professional gambler in Meadow, Kitchener Bowen the Book, was taking small bets favouring Cynlais to win against all comers and at that moment we all agreed with Bowen.

But the sun and all the baked ironies it propagates on this earth were already hard at work. By the time we reached Trecelyn the last petal had dropped from the red rose that Moira Hallam held in her mouth. Moira did her best. She was upset once or twice by Cynlais who in his excitement kept ramming his drum major's staff into her back to remind her that she was not alone. One or two of his thrusts were wild and almost sent Moira hurling into the crowds on the side-walk. Gomer Gough and Uncle

Edwin went on to the road and told Cynlais firmly to cut out this manoeuvre with the staff. Moira kept chewing at the bare stem of her rose and tried to make up for the lack of petals by making more challenging the fine, fluent swing of her body beneath the lovely shawl. Jenks the Pinks had been on the point of making some remark about the lack of stamina of his petals but he just looked at Moira and said nothing. But it was a new band, not much older than our own Matadors, the Aberclydach Sheiks, that did for us in the end.

A few furlongs outside Trecelyn one of our scouts, Onllwyn Meeker, came tearing along the road to give a report on what he had found to Gomer Gough. Onllwyn Meeker had been running hard and he had to be held up and dosed from one of the lemonade bottles that had been brought along for the harder-pressed marchers before he could make a reasonable statement. Meeker was an alarmist and Gomer had been cautioned against making him a scout, and it seemed from the way he shook his forefinger and rolled his eyes that he might well go off the hinge before he managed to tell us what he had seen in Trecelyn.

'Gomer, Gomer,' he said. 'This is a wonderful band you've got here. The Matadors are a credit to Meadow Prospect, but I've just seen the Sheiks of Aberclydach and you've got a surprise coming to you.'

'What's up, Onllwyn?'

'I've just seen them. They're wearing grey veils and dressed like they think Arabs dress in Aberclydach. They're playing some slow, dreamy tune about Araby and swaying from side to side with the music, looking and acting as warm and slinky as you please and promoting a mood of sensuous excitement among the voters.'

'Come on, boys,' said Gomer. 'Let's run ahead and see these Sheiks. I don't like the sound of this. Ephraim Humphries is one of the judges today and by all the rules of nature he should be in favour of the band whose uniforms he helped to buy. But he might well operate against the Matadors on the grounds of discouraging self-pride. And did you hear what Onllwyn said about these Sheiks wearing veils?'

'To keep the sand out of their mouths,' said Onllwyn. 'I was puzzled about these veils and I asked their secretary why sheiks should be wearing veils and he said that about the sand.'

'Ephraim Humphries is going to like the idea of those veils. In everything except his doctrine of damnation for the great majority, he is against the overt. A wholly concealed humanity, beginning with these Aberclydach sheiks, would be quite welcome to Humphries.'

'No doubt indeed,' said Onllwyn Meeker.

'And when he takes a look at Moira Hallam, with that stem in her mouth and the shapes she's making, he'll think she swallowed the petals of that rose herself to keep fresh for some new round of sinning.'

The word 'fresh' seemed to remind Gomer of something and he told Cynlais to break ranks for a few minutes and take a rest on the grass bank that flanked the road.

'They can sit down if they like, but carefully and primly

so that there won't be any creases in the uniform. They've got that old Colonel Mathews the Moloch, the coal owner, on the panel of judges, and they say he's a hell of a man for spotting creases.'

Cynlais passed this warning on to his followers as they were taking their places on the grass bank, and there were a lot of interesting postures.

'There's another thing,' said Uncle Edwin, sucking at two blades of some healthful type of grass that had just been passed to him by Caney the Cure, who was with us as a supporter and because there was never much doing in the herb line during the summer. 'There's another thing. Don't forget Merfyn Matlock.'

'Explain about Matlock,' said Gomer.

Uncle Edwin explained. Merfyn Matlock owned the department store in Birchtown and by the standards of the zone he was a kind of Silurian Woolworth. Merfyn had served in the Middle East with Lawrence of Arabia, dressed as a Bedouin and blowing things up, and he had been flat and sad and bitter ever since he had come back to Birchtown, blue serge and verbal negotiations.

'Remember what he said in 1923.'

Everybody had forgotten what Merfyn Matlock had said in 1923 and Uncle Edwin was asked to remind us.

'We had been having a chat about Matlock and the eager, wolfish way he had of stalking about Birchtown showing contempt for the voters. When he was in the Middle East he believed in explosions in a way that had little to do with the Turks. He made the Bedouin twice as nomadic as they had been before, largely to get out of Matlock's way. So we debated a motion in the Discussion Group that "The shadow of the Boy Scout, with all the attendant ambiguities of his pole, lies too heavily on British society and politics." Many references to Matlock were made in the debate and there was not a single vote against. Matlock commented on this. He said that given a supply of dynamite and a few helpers to keep the matches alight he would deal with the dialecticians of Meadow Prospect in under five minutes.'

'And you say this Matlock is a judge.'

'He is a judge because he is the donor of the silver cup for the best character band. Mathews the Moloch is donating the cash part of the prize.'

'Why not make it plain that we have given up all hard thoughts about Matlock and politics. Why not have a kind of placard carried in front of the band just saying "The Matadors. Above Party. Above Class".'

'Any kind of placard or slogan in front of the band would clash with Moira in that fine romantic costume of hers. But the slogan you've just mentioned would put the judges out for the count. We'll have to rely on the goodwill of Matlock and the others. We'll have to convince them that through these carnivals we are now making our way towards the New Jerusalem by a blither route, thinking no thought that cannot be played on a gazooka. Now, that's enough defeatist talk for one morning. I'm going to get a new rose for Moira. She makes a wonderful picture with that flower hanging from her lips.'

Gomer looked around. The only dwelling on that part of the road was an old cottage in which lived an ancient couple, secluded and somewhat petulant, still closer in spirit to the peasantry of the distant country of their origin than to the loud beetle-browed valleys where they had come tetchily to settle. If they had seen any of the carnivals' bands pass their cottage they had probably taken them as being quite seriously a part of the crudescent lunacy they had always spotted at the heart of the life around them.

In the front garden of the cottage were hundreds of roses in full bloom and of as deep a red as that which had been given to Moira by Jenks the Pinks. If Gomer had had a less sonorous approach to living he could have put his hand over the fence and helped himself to a handful. Instead, he went up the garden path and knocked on the door. The woman appeared and peeped out. She looked as if Old Moore had been keeping her prepared for the coming of Gomer for years. Gomer held out to her the unpetalled stem of Moira's first rose.

'Since the beauty has slipped from this,' he said and gave a light laugh which did not help, 'could I prevail upon you to furnish the lips of Meadow Prospect's Carmen, Moira Hallam, with a rose on a par with that grown by Naboth Jenks the Pinks?'

Every reservation she had ever felt about her days on this earth crowded on to the woman's face. She slammed the door shut and started crying out for her husband, who was somewhere in the back of the cottage. Then the woman's face appeared at one of the front windows, her eyes two pools of shock. A few of Cynlais' matadors, hearing the bang of the door and wondering what Gomer was up to, strolled over the brow of the grass bank and came into view of the cottage. The woman behind the window saw them and the door was instantly locked and barred. Gomer left the garden and picked up a rose on the way.

The band fell once more into line. At the sight of the fresh rose and after a round of servile attendance from Cynlais, Moira had picked up her spirits and the first notes of 'I'm One of the Nuts of Barcelona' had a swirl of optimistic gaiety as the matadors set forth on the last lap of their journey.

'Now let's hurry ahead and see about these Sheiks,' said Gomer.

We reached the centre of Trecelyn at the double. We had passed a group of bands all dressed in chintz, unstitched from looted curtains in the main, and all playing sad tunes like 'Moonlight and Roses', 'Souvenirs' and even a hymn, but those latter boys were wearing a very dark kind of chintz and from their general appearance were out on some subtle branch line of piety. Then we saw the Aberclydach Sheiks and they stopped us in our tracks. What Onllwyn Meeker had said was quite right. The grey veils worn high and seen against the dark, rather fierce type of male face common in Aberclydach, high cheekbones, eyebrows like coconut matting, was disquieting, but in a tonic sort of way. But it was their style of marching that hit the eye. They played the 'Sheik of Araby' very slowly and their swaying was deep and thorough. Their leader, in splendid white robes and a jet black turban about two feet deep and of a total length of cloth that must have put mourning in Aberclydach back a year, was a huge and notable rugby forward, Ritchie Reeves, who in his day had worn out nine referees and the contents of two fracture wards. The drummers also wore turbans but these were squat articles, and it was clear that Ritchie Reeves was making sure that it was only he who would present the public with a real Mahometan flourish. Gomer Gough went very close to the boys from Aberclydach and then turned to us.

'The boys between Ritchie Reeves and the drummers are not sheiks at all. They are houris, birds of paradise, a type of ethereal harlot, promised to the Arabs by Allah to compensate them for a life spent among sand and a run-down economy, but I can see three Aberclydach rodneys in that third row alone who wouldn't compensate me for anything.'

Teilo Dew was staring fascinated at the swaying of our rivals.

'If these boys are right,' he said, 'then the Middle East must be a damned sight less stable than we thought.'

'They are practically leaving their earmarks on either side,' said Uncle Edwin. 'They are wanting to suggest some high note of orgasm and pandering to the bodily wants of Ritchie, who has made it quite plain by the height of his hat that he is the chief sheik.'

We looked at Ritchie. His great face was melancholy but passionate, and we could see that between his rugby-clouted brain and carrying about a stone of cloth on his head his reactions were even more muffled than usual.

'Where are the judges?' asked Gomer, pulling a small book from his pocket.

'Over there in the open bay window of the Constitutional Club.'

We looked up and saw the judges. Right in front was Merfyn Matlock, very broad and bronzed, and smiling down at the Aberclydach band. At his side was the veteran coalowner Mathews the Moloch, and he did not seem to be in focus at all. He was leaning on Matlock and we could believe what we had often heard about him, that he was the one coal owner who had worked seams younger than himself. Behind these two we could see Ephraim Humphries in a grey suit and looking down with a kind of hooded caution at Ritchie Reeves and the houris.

Gomer stood squarely beneath the judges' window, slapped the little book he was holding and shouted up in a great roar, 'Mr Judges, an appeal, please. I've just seen the Aberclydach Sheiks. They are swaying like pendulums and I'm too well up in carnival law to let these antics go unchallenged. The rules we drew up at the Meadow Prospect conference, which are printed here in this little handbook, clearly state that bandsmen should keep a military uprightness on the march. It was with a faithful eye on this regulation that we told our own artistic adviser, Festus Phelps the Fancy, to avoid all imaginative frills that make the movement of the Meadow Prospect Matadors too staccato. And now here we have these Aberclydach Sheiks weaving in and out like shuttlecocks in their soft robes. This is the work of perverts and not legal.'

Merfyn Matlock pointed his arm down at Gomer and we could see that this for him was a moment of fathomless delight. 'Stewards,' he said, 'remove that man. He's out to disrupt the carnival. Meadow Prospect has always been a pit of dissent. Here come the Sheiks now. Oh, a fine turnout!'

We turned to take another look at the Sheiks as they moved into the square and as we saw them we gave up what was left of the ghost. The Sheiks had played their supreme trump. They had slowed their rate of march down to a crawl to confuse the bands behind them. And out of a side street, goaded on by a cloud of shouting voters, came the Sheiks' deputy leader, Mostyn Frost, dressed in Arab style and mounted on an old camel which he had borrowed from a menagerie that had gone bankrupt and bogged down in Aberclydach a week before. It was this animal that Olga Rowe caught a glimpse of as she was led back into position on the square. It finished her off for good.

At the carnival's end Gomer and Cynlais said we would go back over the mountain path, for the macadamed roads would be too hard after the disappointments of the day. Up the mountain we went. Everything was plain because the moon was full.

The path was narrow and we walked single file, women,

children, Matadors, Sons of Dixie and Britannias. We reached the mountaintop. We reached the straight green path that leads past Llangysgod on down to Meadow Prospect. And across the lovely deep-ferned plateau we walked slowly, like a little army, most of the men with children hanging on to their arms, the women walking as best they could in the rear. Then they all fell quiet. We stood still, I and two or three others, and watched them pass, listening to the curious quietness that had fallen upon them. Far away we heard a high crazy laugh from Cynlais Coleman, who was trying to comfort Moira Hallam in their defeat. Some kind of sadness seemed to have come down on us. It was not a miserable sadness, for we could all feel some kind of contentment enriching its dark root. It may have been the moon making the mountain seem so secure and serene. We were like an army that had nothing left to cheer about or cry about, not sure if it was advancing or retreating and not caring. We had lost. As we watched the weird disguises, the strange, yet utterly familiar faces, of Britannias, Matadors and Africans, shuffle past, we knew that the bubble of frivolity, blown with such pathetic care, had burst for ever and that new and colder winds of danger would come from all the world's corners to find us on the morrow. But for that moment we were touched by the moon and the magic of longing. We sensed some friendliness and forgiveness in the loved and loving earth we walked on. For minutes the silence must have gone on. Just the sound of many feet swishing through the summer grass. Then somebody started playing a gazooka. The tune he played was one of those sweet, deep things that form as simply as dew upon a mood like ours. It must have been 'All Through the Night' scored for a million talking tears and a disbelief in the dawn. It had all the golden softness of an age-long hunger to be at rest. The player, distant from us now, at the head of the long and formless procession, played it very quietly, as if he were thinking rather than playing. Thinking about the night, conflict, beauty, the intricate labour of living and the dark little dish of thinking self in which they were all compounded. Then the others joined in and the children began to sing.

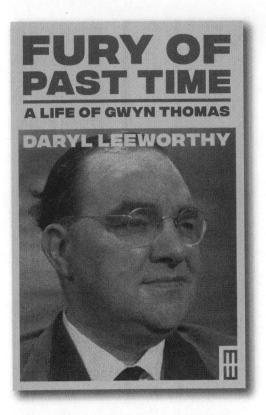

FURY OF PAST TIME:
A LIFE OF GWYN THOMAS
DARYL LEEWORTHY

ISBN: 978-1-913640-10-1
£15.99 | PAPERBACK

"This punchy portrait of a real Welsh literary
heavyweight hits home with the brutal realism of
Thomas' jabbing prose and mordant wit."
– Jon Gower, Nation. Cymru